Cherry Blossom Girls

-Harmon Cooper-

Table of Contents

Chapter One: Dark and Stormy

It was a dark and stormy night when a nude woman showed up on my doorstep.

Really, it was, and sure, calling it *a dark and stormy night* is a literary no-no, but I was a writer – still am, even after all this – and I'm granted at least one hackneyed phrase.

Besides, I wasn't kidding when I said it was dark and stormy. Nor was I kidding about the mysterious nude woman.

The electricity had cut off an hour ago, and a candle that smelled like pipe tobacco was the only thing lighting my tiny basement apartment.

It was cold, and even though I was tucked under a New England Patriots blanket my aunt and uncle had given me for Christmas last year, I could barely feel my toes.

Rain lashed at the tiny slit windows near my ceiling, and the entire apartment building creaked and moaned as thunder boomed in the sky.

Lightning cracked, and just as it subsided, I heard a terrible screech from the street outside.

My attention shifted to the front door as a car horn rang out. The person honked their horn again, and the peeling sound of tires slipped into my apartment.

What's going on out there? I thought as I put my e-reader down.

There was no way for me to look out the window because it was too high up – a basement hopper window – and besides, the window was so grimy on the outside that I wouldn't have been able to see anything anyway.

I had to do something, but …

Like I said before, I was a writer – still am – so I'm clearly not the I-heard-a-sound-outside-better-go-investigate-type.

I didn't have a gun, didn't have any type of survival or Boy Scout training, didn't have any hand-to-hand combat skills, and didn't venture out past dark very often.

Sure, I guess some writers were more daring – your Hemingways and your nature survivalist types … hell, even your gonzo guys – but not a science fantasy writer like me, and especially not a sci-fi writer who wrote gamer fiction.

What's going on out there? I thought as I ran my hand through my beard. More importantly, *Why am I instinctively getting out of bed? Why am I putting my glasses on and smoothing my hands over my sweater?*

A scream outside sent a shiver down my spine.

It was April in New Haven, Connecticut, and it was a lot more frigid than it should have been. I was reminded of this as my bare feet touched the concrete floor and a spark of cold cut into my bones.

I silenced the voice at the back of my head telling me to go back to my bed, get under the covers, finish my digital copy of *The Art of War*, and not venture into the unknown.

I slipped into my sandals and took the steps up to the exit.

The curiosity had gotten to me.

Here goes nothing, I thought as I unlocked the top bolt. I had to see what was going on out there.

A bitter wind fringed with droplets of water nearly tossed me off the steps.

But the weather was of no interest to me as my eyes fell on a naked woman lying on the curb, her skin pale and her long blonde hair a mess over her face.

She looked up at me and her eyes flashed white.

Help.

A feminine voice appeared inside my skull, and my first instinct was to glance around to see where it had come from.

Please ...

The ghastly woman's face began to morph, starting with her bleach blonde hair, which turned dark, and moving down to her chin, which elongated as her skin started to bubble and change color.

Her skin snapped back into place, and she collapsed after one last glance at me with her piercing white eyes.

By this point I was stooped in front of the wet woman, lifting her into my arms.

It was the start of a story that I could have never written, a story that many would later deem impossible, a story that would make my writing famous, and expose a terrible government secret.

She was the first Cherry Blossom Girl.

Chapter Two: You're a Psychic Shifter, and I'm a Terrible Writer

Wooster Square, a small neighborhood near Yale University, was famous for two things.

The first was its pizza, which was remarkable for its taste and the thinness of its crust. The next was the Yoshino Japanese cherry blossom trees, which were planted in 1973 and had thrived ever since, resulting in a yearly festival.

I didn't know the moment I brought the woman into my basement apartment that her arrival would signal the blooming of the cherry blossoms that next morning, but I'd find out soon enough, especially because my apartment was just a few blocks away from the square.

The only thing on my mind as I brought her in and wrapped her in my New England Patriots blanket, was getting her help.

This thought quickly changed when I set her on my bed, and *her face began to change into mine.*

The sheer horror of seeing someone's face change into yours is something I wouldn't wish on my worst enemies. There I was, messy beard, dark bags under my eyes, glasses, hair parted at the side, pointy nose.

It was enough to throw anyone off balance.

I fell backward, cracking my ass on the hard concrete of my floor – dammit, I needed to get to Ikea to get a carpet, but I was broke! – and as I got to my feet, the nude female who had been lying on the curb outside my basement apartment had officially turned into *me*, down to my threadbare sweater.

She stared at me a moment longer and as she touched her face – the spitting image of *my* face – her eyes changed to the same color as mine. Hell, she even had the light beard stubble on the chin and the nonexistent stubble near the corners of my mouth down.

"What the hell are you?" I asked as I backed into my writing desk. My notepad fell, followed by my computer speakers and an old coffee cup filled with pens.

"What the hell are you?" she asked in *my body* but with *her* soft voice.

There was something melodic about the way she spoke, that soothed me even though she was speaking to me from my own body.

"Can you please … um … change back?" I asked.

Change to what?

This time her voice was in my head.

I could have sworn that just moments ago she spoke to me in person … but maybe that was in my head too. My features began to melt away, starting with the crown of her head, and soon she was back to her old self.

Pale skin, bleach blonde hair, blue eyes, voluptuous, clean-shaven – a Scandinavian dream if there ever was one. She didn't seem to mind that she was sopping wet and in a stranger's home. She also didn't seem to mind that the blanket had fallen from her chest, revealing her large breasts.

The candlelight cast her silhouette to the wall on the right, which reminded me that she was indeed a real person. Because for a second there, I thought I'd eaten something bad for lunch, or that the one time I took shrooms in college was coming back to haunt me.

A Joseph Campbell quote came to me: "A blunder – apparently the merest chance – reveals an unsuspected world, and the individual is drawn into a relationship with forces that are not rightly understood."

Ha! I wanted to scream at myself, *if that's not the understatement of the year …*

The electricity flickered on and she looked up to the single bulb hanging from my ceiling.

"Yeah, it's a crappy place," I said.

"Who …?" She pointed at me.

"Who am I?"

13

She nodded, and her voice appeared in my head: *Who are you? Gideon Caldwell? You are Gideon Caldwell.*

"That's right," I told her as I touched my chest. "I'm Gideon."

I hadn't met many people named Gideon, and I doubted that anyone living in Wooster Square was named after someone from the Hebrew Bible. I wasn't raised religious or anything; I think my parents just liked the name because of some song by a band named *My Morning Jacket.*

"I'm Gideon," I said again, with more confidence. "Gideon Caldwell."

Gideon? I like that name.

"How are you doing that, lady?"

She tilted her head at me. "My name isn't lady."

"I have no idea what your name is or what happened, but I'm calling the cops."

I moved to my phone, which rested on its charging pad near my computer.

My legs suddenly stopped functioning.

They didn't turn to jelly or anything, they just froze, as if they'd suddenly been crafted from concrete and left to dry for a week.

My legs frozen, I tried to reach my arms out, but I was too far away from my desk. I looked at the woman as fear spread across my face. I wanted to move, but at the same time, I had the urge to stay exactly where I was.

"You can ... freeze people?"

My knees buckled, and I tumbled sideways, nearly colliding with my lamp.

No call. Her voice whispered inside my head.

"Let me get this straight," I said as I got to my feet. "You can freeze things, talk in my head and ... change forms."

I pinched my arm. *Nope, not dreaming.*

"So," I felt stupid as the next words tumbled out of my mouth. "You're a psychic shapeshifter."

The woman took a deep breath and fell, her head smacking against the edge of my bed and her exposed breasts bouncing up and down.

It must have been something I said.

I tried a few more times to get to my phone with the intent of calling an ambulance.

Every time I moved away from the bed, it became harder and harder to move, as if I were stepping through quicksand, or participating in a mud run. I had a friend who liked to do those mud runs, and I had no idea what the appeal was – nor did I like getting dirty, even though I lived in a kind of grimy basement apartment.

I glanced around. Well, it wasn't too grimy, but it wasn't that nice either.

My computer desk was against the wall next to the door – or I should say, the steps leading up to the door. Next to that were a futon and a small coffee table that I picked up from Goodwill. There was a kitchen, but it was the size of a closet, not even large enough for a microwave. On the opposite side of the kitchen was my bed, and on the opposite side of that was the bathroom.

I liked my bathroom, actually. It had a walk-in shower and an old medicine cabinet. I don't know why I liked that cabinet, but I did.

In less than a week's time, this place would be a distant memory, and my return to New Haven would be tainted by the loss of a friend and an attack from an incredibly powerful super being.

But the Gideon Caldwell a day before the cherry blossoms bloomed had no way of knowing this.

"Remember," I told myself as I paced before the bed, "you're the adult here, um, yeah, you're the adult."

I needed to cool down, and a single aspirin always helped calm my nerves for some reason. I went to the medicine cabinet, took a pill, closed it and looked at my own reflection in the mirror.

"You have to do this."

It was like goddamn Tony Robbins had stepped into the room.

Confidence swelled in me, and sure, I sounded ridiculous, but somehow saying this gave me just enough confidence to go back into my bedroom / living room / kitchen / open area concept space and try to wake the mysterious woman.

Or tend to her.

I didn't have the slightest clue how to 'tend' to someone, but I figured it would involve helping her sit up, or propping her up against a pillow, or putting her feet up – no, no, that was stupid.

I had no idea what I was doing.

Goodbye, Tony! I was nervous, shocked, my palms were sweaty, and I still felt the adrenaline rushing through me. Or at least, the after results of the adrenaline rushing through me.

I had written tons of fight scenes for my LitRPG, cyberpunk, and science fantasy books that I'd self-published to little or no accolades.

One time, I'd received a message from a reader telling me my fight scenes weren't believable, and that adrenaline didn't really make you feel thirsty, or make you feel somehow incapacitated, or make your heart beat so quickly that it felt like it had somehow lodged itself in your throat.

But I just experienced all that, and I knew that what I had written – while maybe a little bit exaggerated – was more or less close to the truth.

I was living proof that the aftershock of adrenaline sucked.

"Why are you arguing with this bad reviewer in your head?" I asked as I returned to the passed-out woman.

The concrete floor was still cold, but I was much more focused on her, and what to do with her, and how she was sleeping yet still preventing me from using my cell phone.

"Superheroes aren't real, magic powers aren't real, shifters aren't real," I told myself.

I tried writing superhero fiction before, but it wasn't that great. I had been too poisoned by Marvel and DC Comics to ever create something on my own, so I scrapped that manuscript. Yet here I was with a possible superhero … or villain?

I glanced at the woman, my heart in my throat again.

Was it really in your throat? a voice inside my head asked, but I ignored that voice because it was really in my throat. I mean, I couldn't feel it, but I could definitely taste blood – wait, no.

No, I couldn't taste blood, but I was definitely shocked, and I definitely didn't know how to react.

"Just breathe, Gideon, just breathe," I told myself. Speaking in third person was a sure sign of insanity. "You can do this, Gideon."

"Please, be quiet," the woman finally said to me. "Your brain is so wild, so … untamed."

"Welcome to being a writer," I said. "Okay, I'm not a great writer or anything, I just wanted to say something clever to you … um, yeah, I'll just be quiet for a moment."

She sat up suddenly, tears streaming down her face.

I dropped to the floor as my thoughts tore out of my head.

It took every ounce of courage not to shriek in agony as my brain pulsed, my eyes bulged, my temples grew to the size of turnips. Something moved through me, razed my inner organs, toasted my medulla oblongata.

"Please, stop," I whispered, pain tearing at my insides. "Please …"

"Sleep," she said, and with those words, I felt my eyes grow tired.

I stood and stumbled forward, propelled by an unknown force.

Quiet, Writer Gideon.

I sat down on the bed next to her and yawned. I could feel her presence next to me even with my drowsiness. My head slouched forward. And I slowly began to lie back onto the bed.

I felt her join me moments later, her wet hair against my chest and neck.

Chapter Three: No Naked Moms in the Morning

"Mom?"

Morning came and with it an absolutely terrifying visual. My fifty-seven-year-old mother stood before me completely naked – breasts hanging off to the side, stretch marks on her belly, an untamed bush, and a gnarly scar from her recent knee surgery.

"What in the fuck?" I shouted, pulling away from her.

It wasn't that I'd forgotten what happened last night, nor the mysterious woman who had shown up at my doorstep; it was more the fact that I'd just woken up and saw my mom standing naked in front of me.

It was an unsettling experience, to say the least.

I was so confused upon waking up to such a sight that I didn't put two and two together and realize it was the shifter, or psychic – or as I quickly recalled, *both.*

"Please … anything but that," I told the mysterious woman, my eyes clenched shut. "Any image but that."

"Does this image disturb you?" she asked in a soft voice.

I nodded. "Just be yourself."

Who knew what 'herself' really was, or what that loaded phrase actually entailed. For all I knew, her Scandinavian features were also just a form she'd taken … that she was actually someone else entirely. Hell, she could even be a man.

That got me thinking about shapeshifters in general and where their exterior features go when they change form.

I never thought about those things when I watched Mystique on the big screen or read comic books about shapeshifters. Hell, even while playing some type of shifter in an RPG, the thought never came to me.

I guess that was the writer in me – the clueless writer, really … because if I had been a better writer or a better observer, I would have probably thought of these things before.

At any rate, I had no idea where exterior body parts like muscle mass and boobage went when a shifter changed forms, and that was probably because shifters weren't supposed to be real in the first place.

"I'm living in a fantasy world," I said, my eyes still shut.

"I changed back."

I slowly peeked my eyes open to see that the woman had changed back to her original form: pale skin, long blonde hair, deep blue eyes.

Of course I took a peek at her other parts – what man wouldn't? – but I tried to keep my gaze at shoulder level and professional.

If you'd asked me the day before, my plan for this morning was to just wake up and write a thousand words or so in my newest book, which I was calling *Breakpoint Online*.

Looking back, the premise wasn't very clever. Basically, a guy trapped in a VR world was forced to team up with his arch nemesis, a mysterious female, in order to free himself – but the story was fresh on my mind, and I had an urge to finish it, just get it done.

What would you like to do to me?

"What would I like to do to you?" I couldn't help but smile at her. "That's a weird question to ask someone when you first meet them. Also, you're speaking in my head again. I'd prefer if you just spoke to me out loud. Is that okay with you? As long as you can speak with your real voice, please just do that. I have enough things zipping around in my mind and stressing me the hell out … like the fact that you've shown up."

"I can go," she said turning to the door.

If you're thinking that I should have let her go to prevent all that was about to happen from happening, you would be correct. If I'd let her go just then, my life wouldn't have changed, I wouldn't have 'broken bad,' and I would have gone on to live a normal-ish New Englander life.

But put yourself in my shoes for just a moment.

I was a twenty-five-year-old guy who worked in what was basically a Yale gift shop (although we sold other things including tchotchkes and for some reason, lamps – lots of fucking lamps), who lived alone, hadn't had a girlfriend in two years, had a hipster beard, and who wrote science fiction for gamers as a hobby.

Now I'm not going to sit here and tell you that I was a loser, because I've met way bigger losers than myself, but I definitely wasn't a winner – which didn't necessarily make me a loser, but it put me pretty close to being one.

"Wait," I called after her. "You can stay but … maybe put some clothes on for a second so I can figure all this out."

Also an amateur move, but having a beautiful nude woman standing before me was distracting, and I needed to get to the bottom of what was going on here.

She agreed and turned to my closet, where she found a button up shirt that was a few sizes too large for her and put it on. She tried on a few of my pants only to realize that they wouldn't fit her very well, which I could have told her if she was paying attention to me.

The thing was, she wasn't paying attention to me in the least bit.

Even as I spoke to her, she just focused on her task of getting dressed, ignoring me entirely.

Eventually, she settled on a pair of sweatpants I'd been meaning to get rid of.

"You should put on some of my underwear too," I told her. I don't know why I told her this, I just figured that everyone should be wearing underwear.

She didn't feel the same way. With my button up shirt over her chest and my sweatpants on, she turned to me and did a little twirl.

"Nice clothes."

I shrugged. "Sorry I don't have any, um, women's clothing, but my uncle's the one into that stuff."

I was trying to be funny, but my humor – however terrible it may be – had little or no effect on her.

She approached me, the movement of her shoulders reminding me of the way a tiger stalks its prey.

I was suddenly nervous seeing her so close to me, and no, I wasn't the type of guy who had never been with a woman before or anything like that, it was just … well, it was all of it.

All of it.

From her sudden appearance in my life to the way she looked at me. I was on pins and needles (another cliché, but fuck it, it worked).

"Let's start with the basics," I told her. "How did you end up on the street last night?"

I couldn't get a sense of the weather outside, but I knew the sun was out, and I knew that the thunderstorm had gone somewhere else, possibly over to Long Island. Good riddance.

"I …" she bit her lip. "I don't know."

"You don't know?"

Something about the way she looked at me betrayed what she'd just said. I sensed it at the time but figured I shouldn't press it.

"Okay then, so what about your abilities? I mean you can change your appearance, and I guess you can change your clothes too, right?"

This made me question if I should have given her any of my clothes or if it would have even mattered.

"Yes." A white kimono with blue flowers cascaded down her body.

I had no idea where she'd seen something like that until I remembered that I had an old painting of a Japanese woman hanging near my bed.

I glanced over my shoulder at the painting to see the geisha in her white kimono with blue flowers to confirm this.

I swallowed hard. "That is something," I said as the white makeup on the woman's face intensified and her deep red lips bloomed with color. "So, you can change into anyone or anything. What about your voice, does your voice change?"

"I don't know." It was the same voice as before. She stood there in her geisha form, her hand on her throat.

"Okay, change back into me, and speak to me." I looked at her curiously for a moment. "You know what I mean."

The woman morphed into my spitting image, even down to my cowlick. She wore the same gray house sweater I currently wore, and the same beard hung from her chin.

"Hi," she said, "my name is Gideon, and I live in a dirty place."

I laughed. While she spoke to me from my body, it was still her soft voice.

It's not that bad, I thought as I cursed myself for leaving a pile of clothes near my writing desk.

"This is a very dirty place." She turned, and for the first time, I saw something on her neck that troubled me.

It was some type of port covered by a small flap of flesh. If she hadn't been in my form, I wouldn't have seen it. The port was just behind her right ear, and as she turned back to me, she noticed that I'd seen it.

"What is that?" I asked.

"I …" Tears began to well in her eyes – *in my eyes*, because she was still in my form. "I don't know."

"Can I touch it?" I asked.

She approached me and sat down on the bed.

Before touching her neck, I touched her sweater. It was hard not to gasp when I found that the texture was spot on.

"That's amazing," I whispered. "It's like you can grow clothes."

"Grow clothes," she said. "I can grow clothes." A dress started to appear on her body, yet she still hadn't changed from my body, which only makes it harder to describe. I'd never worn a dress before, even for Halloween.

"Change back to your original form," I told her.

My face melted away, replaced by her long blonde hair and strikingly beautiful eyes. Her clothes morphed back into the ones she'd taken from my closet earlier, and she moved her hair to the side, craning her neck toward me.

"Is that …" I used my fingernail to push to open the small covering on the port.

I'd never seen this type of technology; it was like they'd fused flesh and plastic to make the covering.

"Do you mind?" I asked as I hovered my hand over her heart. She shook her head and I placed my hand on her chest, feeling her heartbeat. I then checked her pulse. "You're definitely human," I concluded as I returned to the port on her neck and its covering.

"Yes, I'm human."

"It's like the consistency of a callus or something." I popped the cover open.

"What is it?" she asked, her eyes focused forward.

I laughed. "It's a mini USB port. That's … incredibly odd."

It was 2030, and some things still charged using these ports, although most electronics charged wirelessly.

"I can plug you in," I whispered. And my immediate thought – and seriously, blame the gamer and gamelit writer in me for this one – was that I could customize her and adjust her stats.

I quickly replaced this thought with a better, more logical one: *Maybe I can find out more about her if I plugged her in.*

"What are you thinking, Writer Gideon?"

"Writer Gideon, huh? Okay, that name works. I'm thinking we need to plug you in to my laptop. At the very least, maybe we can adjust your shifter voice settings, to make it more believable. Just a hunch."

"And then what?"

"I don't know just yet," I admitted.

"And we can get out of this dirty place?"

"My place isn't that bad, but sure. You're right. We can get out of here. At least I think so. Let me order the cable I need from EBAYmazon. It'll be here in an hour or so; then we can get started."

She looked at the arc of light coming from the windows. "Can we go outside?"

"You mean while we're waiting for the shipment to arrive?" I considered this for a moment. "Sure, but change your form to a different woman, and, um, just don't do anything crazy. No shifting in public."

She changed first to my mother, and I laughed.

"No, not her. Please, stop doing that."

Her form morphed to the geisha on my wall.

"Better, but you'll draw attention with all the makeup and the hairstyle."

The geisha's bun disappeared, and the makeup melted away.

"Yeah, that'll work, but seriously – *no changing forms in public.* At least not yet."

Chapter Four: Shifting in Public

It was a little cold outside, but not too bad. Even if it had been cold, it would have been hard to focus on the weather. As soon as I opened the door to my apartment I was greeted by a sea of cherry blossom trees, truly a sight to behold.

They had bloomed overnight, and the sidewalk was covered in some of the blossoms that had already fallen from the trees. Farther into Wooster Square, people took pictures of the blossoms, posing in front of them. My end of the street was relatively quiet, though. Which would turn out to be a blessing in disguise.

"I really need a name for you," I told the mysterious woman as I continued to take in the scene.

She stood next to me in my clothing but still with her geisha looks. Meaning she looked Japanese or some type of Asian. I wasn't good at identifying Asians, but I had a friend in high school who's from Taiwan who could tell me where any Asian she saw originated from based on their fashion sense and facial features.

But that was beside the point.

I needed something to call her besides 'mysterious woman,' or 'naked shifter who showed up at my door.'

My phone buzzed, and I quickly took it out of my pocket. It was a message from another author I knew, a Canadian fantasy sci-fi author named Luke Lyrian. He mainly wrote paranormal space operas, but he also dabbled in gamelit.

Luke: Hey.

I'd never met Luke in person, but we'd been talking on GoogleFace for like two years now. Funny, that.

"Beautiful looking," the woman whispered as cherry blossoms began to stitch across her sweater.

"Remember, no shifting in public," I reminded her. "And regarding the cherry blossoms, you showed up at the right time. They don't bloom for very long, and if you had shown up a month later, they'd be gone. But like I was saying, what do you want me to call you?"

My phone buzzed again, and I glanced down at it.

Luke: So, I got this cover concept back from my artist. It's just a concept, but I'm loving it. What do you think?

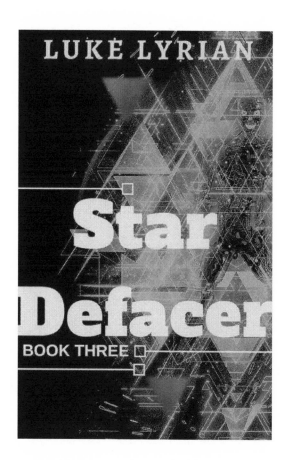

Me: That's fucking sick.

Luke: You like it?

Me: It's ill. Looks good as a thumbnail too. I'd add a bit more texture, maybe something to the title to make it pop. Not that yellow doesn't already pop, but to ground it a little. So, I guess not pop, but give it some character. I like the subtle color change on the author name. I wish I could think of a cool 'Star' title, but I don't want to steal your thunder.

Luke: Plenty of Star titles to go around. It's all about writing to market.

Me: Star Toucher. Star Battler. Star Justice. Star Delvers. Star Online. Star Hammer Online. Paranormal Star Hammerz Online. Star Bastards – that last one was a crazy book, btw. Who would have thought that a dwarf, a goblin, and a gnome would make a killer space trio?

Luke: For sure. That book sold thousands and thousands of copies.

Me: And it spawned so many knockoffs. Star Bitties, Star Kidz, Star Dirt Boys, Star Bistro. Did you read Star Bistro?

Luke: I did not.

Me: It was about a bistro in some galaxy far far away that was taken over by a group of Muslim terrorists. That book got some flack, but the fight scenes were choice.

Luke: I made it through the first two chapters. Yeah, no. Not for me.

"Name ..." the woman said as she touched her face. "I need a name."

"No changing forms," I reminded her. "Just let me message my friend real quick and then we'll go check out the cherry blossoms."

I replied to Luke's last comment.

Me: Hey, do you have a second to video chat?

34

We'd never video chatted before, but I figured it couldn't hurt to ask.

Luke: Driving at the moment. What's up?

Me: I'm going to tell you something that may freak you out just a little bit, FYI.

Luke: Freak me out? Is it a new book? Did you finish Breakpoint Online?

Me: Let's just talk later. Video chat. You're going to want to see this, because when I tell you what I got into last night, you won't believe me.

Luke: Did you have a crazy night or something? Eat too many wings and nachos?

Me: If you only knew ...

"Can we go see the cherry blossoms now?" The woman took a few steps closer to the square.

"That's the plan." I joined her, pocketing my phone. "Also, I need a name from you."

She shrugged.

"Okay, so if you won't tell me a name, how about we come up with an alias for you?"

The woman turned and looked at me, something flashing behind her dark, Asian eyes. A sudden gust of wind whipped strands of her black hair across her face. "What about the name Cherry?" she asked.

I started to laugh.

"What is wrong with this name?"

"It's just kind of a ..."

I was going to say *stripper name* but didn't know if that would offend her. Also, I didn't know if Cherry *was* a stripper name; it just seemed like it might be.

"Never mind, let's just call you Grace."

"Why Grace?" She whispered the name a few more times, touched her chest, considered the name.

"It's the working name for a female character I've been writing for a new series I'm working on."

"Series?"

We stopped in front of one of the cherry blossom trees and I pressed my hand against its trunk. The trunk was cold, still a little wet from last night, and the beautiful bright pink and white flowers above betrayed the coldness of its core.

"I write books," I reminded her. "And I'm working on a series."

"Writer Gideon."

"That's me. And for now, at least until I can figure out who you really are, I'm going to call you Grace."

She nodded. "I like it."

Her face drained of color when two black SUVs appeared on the opposite block. "We need to go back to your place," she said suddenly.

"Why's that?"

Grace pulled at my arm, fear in her eyes as she whispered, "We have to go."

A couple across the street was watching us. "We're drawing attention to ourselves," I said.

Here's the thing: I had no idea what I was doing, nor was I fully aware at the time as to why she'd shown up at my place.

While it is easy in retrospect to put the pieces together and realize that something was terribly wrong – beautiful women don't normally show up at sci-fi writers' doorsteps – I was naive and utterly clueless.

That was, until I saw the utter fear in her eyes.

The two vehicles skidded to a halt, and men *who clearly weren't law enforcement officers* kicked open the door, weapons drawn. They didn't wear typical police uniforms but black outfits with armor up to their necks and visors over their eyes. Tactical suits, with some type of advanced recognition system.

My oh-shit meter went through the roof.

My knees buckled, my heart backflipped in my chest, my mouth went dry, and I began to clam up.

Grace turned to the men, her image wavering as it changed from dressed-down Asian lady back to her true form.

The five men came for her, and as they did, she lifted one hand, curling her fingers in the air as anger spread across her face.

The first two stopped, touched their neck, exchanged glances, and began to choke.

The first man to pass them stopped dead in his tracks, his face contorting under the transparent visor as he began to scream.

He kept screaming and began firing his weapon, which was some type of stunning device, into the cherry blossoms.

The last two men dropped to their knees, took off their visors, and raised their weapons to their heads.

"No!" I shouted as they triggered the weapon, and bolts of electricity took them both down.

I glanced at the couple across the street as the two men fell. Looking left, I saw Grace with one hand aimed at our assailants, and the other hand aimed at the couple.

Her eyes were completely white, her hair starting to rise off her shoulders.

Even though I'd barely moved a muscle, I was out of breath. My hands twitched, and I was surprised to see my legs moving beneath me.

Other people will see us, I thought, remembering that we lived in a dense area with brownstones and apartments that faced the street. Someone was likely watching.

Even with this thought at the back of my skull, and knowing that it wouldn't be very difficult to locate me, I returned with her to my basement apartment.

In retrospect, we should have got the hell out of there – out of Connecticut, even out of America – but I was still new at this, and panic had clouded my thinking capabilities.

"Who's after you?" I asked as we reached my apartment. I fiddled with the key, opened the door, and together, we ran down the steps into my dingy apartment.

Grace stood near the door with her hands at the ready, watching the opening intently, waiting for someone to come through.

If you listed all the things a noob would do in this situation, I would pass with flying colors. If it were a test, I would fail miserably.

But I eventually got my bearings, and as I did so, I started to put the pieces of this puzzle together.

Mysterious woman shows up on doorstep? Check. Some type of law enforcement agency after her, likely federal? Check. A little bit of amnesia? Definitely. A possible government conspiracy? Get out your tin hats. Danger for Yours Truly? You bet. But as Gabriel Garcia Marquez said in *Love in the Time of Cholera,* "Wisdom comes to us when it can no longer do any good."

Somehow, I had found myself in either a) an urban fantasy or b) the start of a superhero story.

Except I wasn't a superhero, and the shifter psychic with me didn't seem like a superhero. She'd just attacked the feds, or at least people I assumed were federal agents.

But is she a villain?

And this begged the question:

Does the opposite of superhero always have to be villain?

"Quiet, Writer Gideon, your mind is on fire," she said, her eyes trained on the door.

"Who are those people?" I asked. I could feel the color return to my face.

I was frightened – hell, I was scared shitless and witless – but I was also intrigued, and part of me knew that with what she'd already shown me, it would take quite a bit of manpower to take her down.

"They're after me."

The next question was stupid, but I had to ask it anyway. "Are you a mutant?"

She turned to me as a smile crept up her face. "Not like the mutants in your head."

The mutants in my head? Yep, she'd read my thoughts again, and likely stumbled upon a preteen fascination with X-Men.

"Sorry, dumb question," I told her. My phone buzzed. "You've got to be kidding me," I said as I looked at a prompt from EBAYmazon telling me that my package had been dropped off. Damn them and their fast delivery!

"Looks like we have a package."

She only nodded.

"The package may help us."

If I could plug her in, I'd likely be able to figure out a little more about what was going on here. But that might give our location away. Unless …

I moved over to my computer and unhooked the Wi-Fi. Again, an amateurish move that I should have made last night. But I was trying, and that's all that counts.

A few thoughts came to me rapid-fire.

First, my basement apartment would not do, at least not for much longer.

We only had one exit, and that exit let out onto the street, which meant that we were trapped and could easily be taken out with, say, a smoke bomb. Or whatever else a government agency trying to capture someone who's *not* a mutant, yet has mutant powers, would use.

I'm not a mutant, her voice said in my head.

"Yeah, I know, I'm just thinking things through, and no talking in my head."

Your second idea is better. Plan B.

I hadn't even gotten to my second idea, and the fact that she knew what it was only made me more nervous to be around her.

Could she read my future thoughts? Could she immediately understand and interpret my sudden desires?

She didn't answer that one, thank Jeebus.

So, I started prepping for Plan B by packing a duffle bag.

I grabbed my laptop and its charger, some clothes, my passport, any documents that I thought were necessary including my birth certificate and my social security card. Yep, I still didn't quite realize the seriousness of my situation – that these documents would prove useless to me after what I'd do later – but like I said, I was still getting used to this breaking bad thing.

Once I had my shit packed, I ordered a self-driving UberLyft to pick us up. I knew we'd be trackable, but at least we could make it a little harder to find us, which was part two of Plan B: using Grace's abilities to our advantage.

If people were after us, and if we were going to fight for our lives, we might as well go out in style.

I actually thought this at the time, which was odd for a semi-reclusive bearded writer guy like me. But a little voice at the back of my head told me it was the right thing to think, and as I'd later find out, that voice belonged to Grace.

Chapter Five: Adjusting Grace's Stats

If you imagine me peeking out into the streets holding a broom with the hope of braining one of the Agent Smiths – I still, at this point had no idea what to call them – then you wouldn't be far off.

I didn't have a broom, but I did have a duffle bag and a hunting knife my uncle gave me – yes, the cross-dressing one. I also had a broom, but this was mostly so I could try to scoot the EBAYmazon package away from the stoop to a more reachable location.

Damn USPS never delivered my packages correctly, preferring to leave them on the stoop. A stoop accessible by anyone passing.

But I'd gotten lucky, and the package was relatively easy to reach. The mini USB cable was in a yellow envelope, wrapped in plastic bubble wrap. Knowing I didn't have time to really play around with it, I stuffed it in my duffle bag.

Behind me, Grace placed a hand on my shoulder, and my nerves tingled.

It took us all of five minutes to rip my apartment apart. It was her idea, to make the grimy place dirtier, and I obliged.

"I can't believe I'm doing this," I said for probably the tenth time.

"You'll get used to it."

I've never been the type that would just set everything down and go off on an adventure, but I was twenty-five now, and I worked at a fucking Yale gift shop. I had a BA in Comparative Literature from the University of Southern Connecticut, and I hadn't had a girlfriend in years.

If ever there was a time to abandon it all, now was that time.

All this to say: I fucking destroyed my computer with a hammer.

My work was saved in the cloud anyway, and having seen Grace use superpowers, I knew that whatever happened from this point forward *would not* involve my shitty basement apartment.

"Here goes nothing," I whispered as the self-driving UberLyft pulled up to the curb.

As we climbed into the car, I glanced around to see that all signs of the 'security' team from earlier were gone – *poof* – as if they'd never existed in the first place.

The thought came to me: *Am I being too extreme about this? Should I just lay low for a while?*

But, as Henry Miller once famously wrote in *Tropic of Cancer*, "There are people who cannot resist the desire to get into a cage with wild beasts and be mangled."

If there was a quote to define my life going forward, it was this one.

As a drop off point, I'd chosen a three-star hotel in East Haven near the Long Island Sound. We were definitely going to get out of Connecticut, but I wanted to spend some time trying to figure out what Grace was and why she was on the run before we hit the open road for good.

The UberLyft curved to the on-ramp as Grace scooted closer to me, and her arm immediately wrapped around mine.

We knew not to speak in the UberLyft, just in case we were being recorded, and I hoped our disguises would at least help us find cover for long enough to get our bearings.

She'd chosen to become a cute redhead with glasses and a smattering of freckles across the bridge of her nose. A tight pantsuit and high heels completed her outfit.

I didn't have a great disguise, but I did have a Yale baseball cap and a pair of fake Wayfarers on for good measure. I also wore a scarf around my neck that I'd tugged up to the bottom of my beard.

Grace laid her head on my shoulder and looked up at me.

I wanted to hug her in that moment, to share my apprehension of the choices we'd just made, but I kept my composure, focusing on the cars around us instead.

Keep your cool, Gideon, I reminded myself, like it somehow mattered.

By stepping into this UberLyft, I'd made my decision. There was no turning back.

We arrived at the hotel and the vehicle dropped us off in the back, as per my instructions. We waited for the UberLyft to leave before speaking.

"I'm counting on you," I told her, "and your abilities."

She nodded. "What do I say again?"

"I want you to tell the person at the front desk that we have a reservation. Make them think it has been paid for and that our names are … Edward and Jill King."

"Edward and Jill King."

I could tell by the glint in her eyes that she knew what to do but that she too needed some reassurance. I would later learn this about her and the other one like her: even with their great powers, they still needed reassurance; they still needed to be reminded sometimes of just how strong they were.

We entered the lobby, Grace still a redhead. There were a couple of fake plants, a television broadcasting some shitty local newscast, a coffee bar with a Keurig machine, and a lime green sofa. Tasteful.

After smoothing her hands over her dress, Grace stopped in front of the receptionist's desk and told the lady what we'd gone over.

"Edward and Jill King ..." The receptionist took a moment to scroll through a list of scheduled guests. "I don't see you here. Did you make the reservation online?"

"We sure did," I told her.

"Yes, we made it, um, online," said Grace.

A look of confusion followed by sudden understanding smoothed over the receptionist's face. She nodded, prepared the room key, and told us about checkout and free continental breakfast in the morning.

"Enjoy your stay," she called after us.

"That was awesome," I told Grace as soon as we'd gone up the elevator and found room 224.

"Really?" she asked, turning to me. It was like she'd never been complimented before; she wasn't quite confused, but she didn't smile nor offer any indication that she appreciated admiration.

"Really."

I scanned the keycard and the door popped open. Whoever had cleaned the place went overboard on the air freshener, which made me wonder what the hell had gone on in here the previous night.

I set my duffle bag on the floor and got my laptop out.

Once I plugged in the cable, I moved over to the bed.

"Lay down," I told Grace as I booted up my machine.

"Okay."

The receptionist had given us a single room with a king-size bed. Grace's decision or the receptionist's? Who knew.

My phone buzzed, and I saw that it was a message from Luke. I ignored it for the moment, so focused I was on plugging into Grace's neck and seeing what I could discover.

I wasn't disappointed.

Grace rested with her hands on her chest, the mini USB cable plugged into her neck.

"Okay, here goes nothing," I said as I plugged the other end into my laptop.

A shadow box appeared.

[Initiating user]

[Anonymous User Y/N?]

I thought about that for a moment. If I selected 'yes,' then it may trigger some alarm that gives off her location. If I selected 'no,' then

I'd likely have to log in somehow, and I for sure didn't have any login ID.

"It's asking me if I'm an anonymous user," I told her. "Do you know anything about this?"

"No."

"Okay." I thought some more. "If I say I'm not an anonymous user, do you think you could help me find a password? Surely some part of you knows who installed this or was around when someone plugged into the port in your neck."

She tilted her chin and looked down at me, an indecipherable expression on her face.

"Well?"

"Username: 1351885. Password: 1QAZ2WSX3EFV4321QWEASD."

"Um, shit. That was awesome, Grace."

"Thank you, Writer Gideon."

I bolted to the room's desk and found a pen and a hotel notepad. I asked her to repeat the details, and as I wrote them down, I got to wondering if it was caps or lower-case letters. I asked, but she didn't quite understand what I meant.

[Anonymous User Y/N?]

Here goes nothing, I thought as I selected 'N.' The username and password screen popped up. I typed the username and tried the password in all caps.

It worked.

An hourglass appeared on my desktop. It began doing the AppleSoft spin, the sand moving from one side of the hourglass to the other as it processed. My laptop whirred, the fans kicking into gear.

It was risky; I wasn't foolish enough to believe that what I was doing wouldn't end up triggering some type of built-in locator and getting us caught.

But curiosity killed the cat, and many times it also killed your favorite writer.

Or something like that.

My curiosity paid off when a program opened after a few more seconds of loading. There were file folders – old school style with a plus sign that opened the drop-down menus. A ton of folders, actually, and even more subfolders.

"How is it?" she asked.

"Just getting in. This may take me a couple minutes."

"I'm hungry."

"Me too, actually," I said as I continued to click through folders and subfolders.

I'd been so shocked to wake up and see my naked mother before me that I forgot to eat breakfast. Just thinking about food made me feel like my blood sugar dropped.

"Okay, we'll order a pizza, and when they get here I need you to work your mojo."

"My mojo?" she asked, tilting her head toward me again.

"Don't turn your head too much, and by your mojo, I meant your special abilities."

"Should I change my form?"

"No, I mean your mind abilities." I stopped scrolling through folders and looked over at her. "We don't have any cash, and I don't want to use my cards at the moment. Just in case we're being tracked."

"Okay," she said, confusion still evident in her voice.

"Trust me."

"I'm hungry."

"I'll order the pizza now and get back to checking the files. Just hang for a moment; close your eyes, relax."

"Okay, Writer Gideon."

I was about to order a pizza with my phone, when I figured that would be traced back to me. So I decided to do something Gen Z rarely did. I moved to the phone near the bed, read the Wendy's Hut pizza sticker on the phone, called the number, and placed an order to be paid upon delivery.

They asked me for a credit card, but I was able to weasel my way out of it by saying that I didn't have one, that I was kind of an off-the-grid guy, but that I did have a hotel room. I gave him the hotel information from the notepad, just in case they wanted to have the hotel charge me.

I assured them I had cash a couple more times and they obliged.

"When they get here, I'll tell you what to say before we open the door, okay?"

"Okay."

"Now, let's see what I can figure out here," I said as I returned to my laptop.

I scrolled down the list of available folders and quickly found a folder with the same code she'd told me earlier: 1QAZ2WSX3EFV4321QWEASD. I checked the number I'd written on the piece of paper and clicked it.

A new shadow box appeared.

Build: 008

Base height: 181 Centimeters

Base weight: 54 kilos

I scrolled through this information, not too keen on figuring out her bust size and the other details it listed.

I found a section about abilities and clicked to a submenu.

Main: Psychic

* Omnikinesis, Level 1

* Second Sight, Level 1

* Psychometry, Level 5

* Telepathy, Level 8

* Clairsentience, Level 7

* Psychokinesis, Level 1

* Hypnosis, Level 6

"Shit …" I said as I finished reading through her main abilities.

Each of them allowed me to click and explore further, but the next screens were grayed out and slightly blurred. From what I could tell in the grayed-out section, there were toggles, meaning …

"You're customizable," I gasped.

"Okay," she said, still staring up at the ceiling.

"And I'll hurry, Grace; we have all day to play around with this."

"It's fine. I'm hungry."

"Pizza is coming. Ever had pizza?"

"No."

"You'll love it."

I scrolled back to the main folder under abilities and clicked on it.

There wasn't much information, but I was able to modify the options, unlike her psychic abilities. They were also presented differently, with little dials next to them that I could adjust. All aside from 'Voice Match,' which was already at its highest level.

Main Second: Shifter

Speed of Change: 10

Texture Consistency: 10

Opacity: 10

Voice Match: 2

"Ah, that's where it is ..." I clicked the 'Voice Match' dial and turned it up to ten.

"Did you find something?" she asked.

"I want you to change into my form, and speak to me in my voice."

Her face began to melt away, and from the center of the melting point, my face began to take shape. My auburn hair, my beard, my glasses, my slight Adam's apple, and the rest of my body.

55

The only thing that made it odd – aside from every part of what was going on at the moment – was the fact that she was still wearing women's clothing.

"Okay, say something."

"Something," she said in my voice.

At least I assumed it was my voice. As Chuck Klosterman once famously asked, "How do we tell the difference between an instrument and its sound?"

"That is crazy, seriously crazy. And I just realized that I don't really know what my own voice sounds like," I finally said. "So, can you change into another shape – something different from your base form?"

"Sure." She began to change into the receptionist we met downstairs. The receptionist was a black woman, maybe in her early thirties, with curly hair and a birthmark on the side of her neck.

"How's this look?" she asked in the woman's voice.

"That is so awesome, I can't even begin to describe how awesome that is."

An idea came to me. I moved to the flat screen television and turned it on manually. It was a newscast, with a stern-looking man in a suit and tie reporting on the financial markets.

She tilted her head down just a little bit, and the light from the television flashed across her eyes.

"Can you change into him?"

It only took her a moment to completely transform her body into the man on the television, even down to the pin on his lapel.

"Say something."

"Something."

"Okay, funny joke. Say something else; tell me about your day."

"I woke up today in the house of a strange man named Writer Gideon," she said in the newscaster's voice. "Except it wasn't a house, it was a dirty apartment. I looked in his mind for a minute and changed into his mother, which he doesn't like. We went outside and saw the beautiful cherry blossoms. Then we were attacked. We came to this hotel, ordered pizza – I'm very hungry – and Writer Gideon played around with my settings."

"That's so weird," I started to say. Instead, I said, "Okay, next test. Can you change into an object?"

"An object?" she asked, her manly brows furrowing.

"Like a table."

"No."

"An animal?"

"No."

"Can you change on command?"

"What do you mean?"

"Change into an Asian woman."

She turned back into the Geisha form that she'd taken in my bedroom / living room / kitchen / home.

So, she has to see it, or have seen it, to change into its form. But what about my mom?

"I saw your mom in your head," she told me.

"Reading my thoughts. That's right, you're good at that."

"I didn't speak inside your head this time."

"You're right, you didn't, and thanks for that." I returned my focus to the laptop and looked at the other options. One thing I wanted to play around with was the opacity, which seemed kind of strange to me.

"You can change back into your base form now," I told her.

Boom.

The Scandinavian beauty was back, her hair long and flowing, her eyes light blue, her skin crystal clear, and her large chest visible under my loose clothing. I don't know what part of me liked the fact that she was still wearing my shitty clothing, but there was something kind of sexy about it.

It reminded me of my ex, when she'd stay over and sleep in my stuff.

"Don't do it," I told her as her face started to split and morph into my ex's face.

A tight smile took shape on her face.

"Yeah, you know how to push someone's buttons, I'll give you that."

"You're pushing my buttons," she said, using her eyes to point at the laptop.

"We're going to try something," I said. "So relax and let's see what happens here."

I adjusted the opacity down, and to my other horror, she began to fade away until she was completely invisible.

"That's not fucking possible," I whispered as I reached out for her. I could still touch her, but if I set the opacity at one, I couldn't see her. "I can turn you into a ghost?"

"A ghost?"

I returned the opacity to its normal level and she reappeared.

"Yeah, let's just, um, not get too crazy with that one yet."

There were a ton of things I wanted to test, including using my cell phone to adjust her stats. I knew I'd need a mini USB to mini USB to do that, but it was something I could get later. Further, there were all those other folders.

"Can I rest for a moment?" she asked, just as I was about to perform some new tests. "I'm hungry."

"Sure, let's eat, and then go from there." I unplugged the cable from her neck and put my laptop up.

On the TV, the newscaster was still rambling about the stock market.

"Come up here," Grace told me as she sat up and leaned back against the headboard.

"Don't mind if I do."

Chapter Six: Stolen Pizza and the Idea of a Lifetime

"Remember what I told you," I said to Grace as she approached the door. She held a piece of paper in her hand, and as she adjusted her blouse, her hair slicked back and darkened.

"Hello," she said as she opened the door.

I could tell by the guy's scratchy voice that he was in his teenage years, but I didn't feel too bad ripping him off. I was already beyond that, already knew that I'd crossed the threshold between outstanding citizen and future grifter.

Well, I guess I was never ever an outstanding citizen, but at least I've never stolen anything or tried to rip anyone off. Scratch that – I did steal my Yale hat from the gift shop I worked at. But that was beside the point.

"Chicken and spinach, correct?" the teen asked.

"Yes, and here is your money," she said in a sweet voice; stilted, but sweet. "I also left a little for a tip."

"Um ..."

I felt my tension grow, but I ignored it. I knew she could do it, and I had the feeling if she *couldn't* do it, she could simply fry his mind.

"Enjoy the pizza," he said as the door shut.

"You didn't tell him to pay for the actual pizza with his own money?" I asked her. "Remember, the paper was just a decoy."

She opened the door and called after him. "Where is your money?"

I cringed. If she didn't have control over his mind, that would have been one hell of a question to ask.

"In my wallet."

"Okay. Go to your car. Use money from your wallet to pay for the pizza. Thanks!"

"No problem, enjoy," he said.

Grace turned to me, a huge smile on her face.

The incredibly delicious scent of pizza had already drifted over to me, and my mouth was watering by the time she brought it to the bed.

"Be careful with the pizza," I reminded her. "It's pretty greasy." I opened the box and went for my first slice.

"I don't mind." She stuffed a slice in her mouth. Cheese dripped from her chin and she lifted her hand to wipe it off.

I laughed.

"What?" she asked with her mouth full.

"It was cute, that's all," I said around my own mouthful of pizza.

"I'm eating, and it is cute?"

"Never mind." I took another bite.

We returned our focus to the television. There was a movie on now, an action flick with a famous Hollywood star named Natalie Johansson. I looked from Natalie Johansson on the screen, wearing a torn tank top and a submachine gun tucked under her arm, to Grace.

"Can you …?"

She swallowed her pizza and her face morphed into a splitting image of Natalie Johansson. From there, and as she took another bite, her body began to change until she wore the exact same clothing that Natalie wore in the movie.

"I just don't know what to say about stuff like that, to be honest with you."

It was strange, it was amazing, it was utterly fantastic, cool, unique, powerful, and I wasn't going to say I was in love, but I was definitely moved.

We finished our pizza. Once we were done and I started cleaning up, I realized that we were both thirsty.

I wasn't paying attention earlier when I ordered the pizza; I should have gotten the pizza and drink combo, or whatever the hell they had

63

at the time. Unfortunately, we were stuck with what was in the hotel bar …

Which just happened to be alcohol.

"I think I'm going to have a drink of something," I told her.

"I would like a drink of something as well," she said. While her voice was sweet and soft, the way she spoke was very robotic. Which made sense; she was clearly some type of lab experiment – someone who had been sheltered from the masses, hidden away and possibly kept in isolation. They would have had to be careful with her, especially with the powers she possessed.

"Have you ever drunk alcohol?" I asked her.

"Nope, what's that?"

"Let's just stick to cola for now." I approached the bar and took one of the sodas out. I found a glass, poured it up and gave it to her.

She took her first sip and threw the glass to the floor, anger spreading across her face.

"Hey!"

"What was that?" she asked with fear in her eyes, her hands on her throat.

"Whoa, whoa. Don't throw drinks in the room, please. Seriously. It was just soda."

"Soda? You said it was cola."

"You've never had …" I considered this. Never having cola and then having some *would* be pretty weird. "Did you at least like the taste?"

"No. Water."

I returned to the mini fridge. "There's a bottle of water in here too. Have that."

"And alcohol? Can I have alcohol?"

"How old are you?" I asked, which sounded stupid less than a millisecond after leaving my lips. Maybe I should have paid more attention to her bio when I looked through her file. She had to be somewhere between eighteen and twenty-two. She didn't look much older than that, and I hoped she wasn't younger. I quickly changed my line of questioning. "I mean, do you know what alcohol is?"

She shook her head.

"Then, maybe you shouldn't have alcohol, just yet."

"Okay," she said, the robotic cheer returning to her voice. "And I'm twenty-one, by the way."

The urge to write is strong with this one, and that 'one' was me. I was dying to sit at my keyboard for a little bit and just pour my thoughts out. *Breakpoint Online,* however cliché a title, wasn't going to write itself, and I could tell by the way Grace was yawning, that she was feeling a nap coming on.

While I would have liked to hook her up to the laptop and probe a little longer – a strange sounding sentence, but you know what I mean – I also wanted to let her rest. After all, whatever she'd been through the previous night had been pretty traumatic. Traumatic for me as well.

My phone vibrated again, and I glanced at it. It was another message from Luke, and in looking at my phone, I suddenly realized that I'd had my GPS on this entire time.

You are such a fucking noob! I thought as I toggled the GPS off and read Luke's message.

Luke: Hey, I'm available now. What did you want to show me?

A couple of hours ago, I would have happily live-streamed everything that was happening and blown Luke's mind. I would have freaked him out by asking Grace to turn into him – which would have made him want to fly down here from Canada – and *I would have also blown my cover.*

And I didn't have a lot of cover to blow, especially since I'd had the GPS on this entire goddamn time.

So, I decided to play it cool this time.

Me: Hey what's up?

Luke: You tell me.

Me: Nothing much, just about to sit down and write some Breakpoint Online. I showed you the cover, right?

Luke: Not bad. Only thing I'd change is the tint and the blur between the lightning and the bottom half. Also, make her have a hood. You definitely want a hood. All the best-selling covers have someone in a hood. I don't know why wearing a hood suddenly makes a book better than a hoodless covered book, but c'est la vie. We must feed the beast, and the beast is the reader!

Me: Sweet, thanks for the feedback. I'll work with it.

Luke: How far in are you again?

Me: I am not too far in, TBH. Maybe about 11k, something like that.

Luke: How's the pacing going? Did you introduce the antagonist yet? Are things starting to heat up, or are you still working on the build-up? First or third person?

Me: I think I'm still working on the build-up. First person, pacing seems fine. Maybe going a little too fast, in my opinion, but readers dig that.

I glanced over at Grace, who had laid her head down and was breathing lightly, her eyes closed.

Luke: Sounds interesting, buddy. I can't wait to read it. I mean, if it's as cool as your last one ...

Me: How Heavy This Axe continues to be my best seller. This new one is definitely cool, and it ...

As Grace yawned, an idea came to me; a way I could talk about what was happening without revealing the truth to Luke.

Me: The book's premise centers around a psychic shifter who shows up in the main character's life, seemingly out of nowhere.

Luke: Shifter? I didn't expect it to involve something like that, you usually write sci-fi, not paranormal romance shit.

Me: Lol. It is not exactly paranormal romance, but there definitely is a psychic shifter involved.

Luke: And is she a ghost?

I thought of Grace's ability to turn completely transparent.

Me: In a way, but it's not paranormal. Maybe it's more superhero-ish.

Luke: Okay, I'm hooked, tell me more.

Me: That quick, huh?

Luke: Lol. As long as it isn't paranormal romance.

Me: I'm not selling out, dammit! Okay, so the book starts on a dark and stormy night, when this guy is just chilling in his apartment and this random woman shows up.

Luke: And is she naked?

Me: Yeah, she's naked.

Luke: Sexy?

Me: Incredibly.

Luke: Okay, that'll be a way to start a story, at least you'll get people to the second chapter.

Me: Well, that was the plan.

Luke: And then what happens next?

Me: She shows him that she's a shifter by turning into him, and after some confusion, they eventually go to sleep.

Luke: I see a hole in the plot.

Me: Hit me.

Luke: Wouldn't he just call the cops if a naked woman showed up at his doorstep? Especially if she was a shifter. She doesn't threaten him or anything, does she?

Me: Nope, not a plot hole, but she won't let him call the cops. Or call anyone. She will let him call for pizza, but that's later. She uses her psychic abilities to prevent him.

Luke: Ooo... she has a secret!

Me: Definitely.

Luke: Okay, what happens next? Do you have an action scene or something that gets things going after that initial kind of shock intro?

Me: Yeah, I do. They go outside the next day and run into some government security guard type guys with advanced weaponry. Black armor, mil-spec shit. You know the drill.

Luke: I love advanced weaponry!

Me: Hell yeah, you do. That gun crafting system you used in Star Defacer was legit AF. Anyway, she uses her powers to stop them, which really kick-starts everything.

Luke: Oh man, that sounds fun. I don't know what I would do in that situation.

Me: Well, I had the protagonist decide to throw it all away and just join her and whatever escapades she was about to get them both into. Break bad.

Luke: Break bad!

Me: So they go to a hotel, and she uses her psychic abilities to trick the receptionist into thinking they booked a room. Then they order pizza.

Luke: That's it?

Me: Then he realizes he can plug into her neck and modify her stats.

Luke: Ah, the LitRPG element. Better put that in. People love that shit. Crunchy or light?

Me: Light, so maybe more gamelit.

Luke: Give the people what they want! Does he have sex with her?

Me: Not yet.

Luke: Might as well make that happen sooner or later. I mean, some of my fans prefer if I hold back, but it sounds like you got a chance for sex going there, and you'd better introduce some of that soon. Besides, who wouldn't want to have sex with a shifter? That'd be crazy.

Me: Working on it.

Luke: So, what did you want to show me? You wanted to video chat earlier ...

All the blood rushed to my head.

It was a cool idea. It was my best idea. And it was actually happening to me at that very moment.

Plus, there was something else going on, some bigger government conspiracy – *definitely a government conspiracy* – and this story needed to get out there. If other people were going through the same thing, they could hear about the story, and maybe we could connect in some way.

I would publish all this. My next manuscript would be about what was currently happening to me. And I'd continue to talk to Luke about it, under the guise that I was working on *Breakpoint Online.*

Me: Luke, you're brilliant.

Luke: Me? Thanks, buddy. But what did you want to talk about?

Me: My new idea, which we've just discussed. Looks like Breakpoint Online is going to be a sweet book. I'll need to change the title at some point, but that's fine.

Luke: I'm totally excited to hear where it goes.

Me: As am I.

Luke: Cool, well I have some editing to do. We'll talk soon! Remember: action, action, action. That's what this crowd is after, lol.

Me: I'm sure action is coming in the next chapter or so. Thanks for the advice, and happy editing!

Chapter Seven: Data Breach

Three thousand words wasn't bad, and it had only taken me about an hour and a half to write them. I could have written more, but as I started the next portion, Grace began to stir.

She yawned and turned to me with a smile on her face. Not as tight as it had been before, as if she had really started to relax some and come to grips with our new life together. Weird saying it like that, but we really were in it together by this point.

"Are you ready to do some more sleuthing?" I asked.

"Sleuthing?" She scooped her hair out of her face. In an instant, her features were perfect; she no longer looked like she'd just woken up from a nap. I guess that was one advantage of being a shifter.

"Did you use your abilities to make it look like you'd just woken up from a nap?"

She shrugged.

"That is an entirely inventive way to use shifter abilities. Anyway, do what you have to do, and we'll get started."

She took this to mean use the restroom. The question was: Did she intuit this, or did she read my mind? There was no way of telling, nor would there ever be a way for me to know if she was reading my mind or not. As we later grew closer, this would continue to be an issue for us.

Grace returned and lay on the bed, angling her neck toward me again.

Once I plugged her in, I went through the same login procedure and soon, I was in.

"There's so much here," I said as I perused the files. Many of them only linked to one or two subfolders, most of which contained binary data and other info that I couldn't parse. I found some quotes from books, some past weather information, and a bunch of other random shit.

Where's the good stuff? I thought as I continued to click through folders.

It was nothing like the movies, where some guy just hacks in and finds exactly what he was looking for. Nor was I typing like a madman as information splashed across the screen, my face lighting up a la Edward Snowden as I perused government data.

But I continued to dig, just like an archeologist, and eventually, I stumbled upon a folder that had some of the contract info between …

Yale and the FCG?

Jackpot.

There wasn't a lot of detail there, but I could tell that whatever program Grace had taken part in, and the program that had given her the powers she possessed, was most definitely funded by the FCG in conjunction with Yale's newly remodeled Rose-Lyle facility.

The FCG, or Federal Corporate Government, was part of a government rebranding effort in the 2020s, especially after the fake news era had passed and the government took this to mean that people wanted unrestricted transparency.

So, they called it what it had become: the Federal Corporate Government. And while I was old enough to remember when it was just the American Government, I found myself using the acronym from time to time as well. It also coincided with lower corporate tax rates, to the sweet tune of ten percent, and another tax hike on the middle class.

I imagined my writer buddy, Luke, telling me to cool it with the backstory at this point, but really, if he could have seen what I was looking through – dozens of contracts with both the FCG, vendors, a private security company called MercSecure, as well as some of the reports – he'd feel the urge to mansplain as well.

Again, this wasn't some complex Dan Brown all-the-way-up-to-the-Vatican type of conspiracy novel. I mean, it was pretty much textbook at this point: a superpowered woman who was part of a secret government and university funded experiment escaped from captivity and showed up at my doorstep.

This got me thinking about the difference between superhero powers and magic powers.

Didn't the X-Men and all the DC Comics people and Marvel heroes and heroines simply have magic powers? I mean, not Batman, of course, and a few of the other ones like Tony Stark, but what was the real difference between a magic power and a superhero power? Why did we feel the urge to differentiate?

At any rate, it didn't matter now, and I could parse through all this later and debate with the voice in the back of my head until I got tired of listening to my own shit.

What mattered was that I uncovered something big.

And I mean really big.

The first discovery came to me in a subfolder of a subfolder, so a sub-subfolder.

There are others.

I found pictures of a dozen or so test subjects, and two, in particular, stood out to me. One resembled Grace, yet she had shorter hair and a much fiercer face. The other was a man with long black hair and an incredible physique.

After a little more digging, I found pictures of Grace as a young girl and wondered if she had a mother. The reason I wondered this was because of some of the scientific papers I'd found in this collection, which talked about growing a fetus in a lab and creating a superhuman or super soldier type of person.

I know, I write science fiction, and I should be better at describing these things, but in my defense, all my science fiction was bullshit. This stuff was real, and I didn't have a photographic memory – aside from when it came to book quotes – nor was I quickly able to interpret scientific papers that broke things down to the molecular level.

But I got the gist.

And that could have been the end of the story if I hadn't stumbled upon a photo of myself.

I gasped as I saw a picture of me taken when I was about five years old.

It was me. I knew it was me. I could tell by the cowlick and by the eyes. I mean, who doesn't recognize themselves as a child?

"What the fuck am I doing in here?" I mumbled.

I wasn't paying attention at the time, but had I been looking at Grace, I might have seen her smile a bit.

No, I was too focused on clicking my photo, clicking through to whatever I could find about the test subjects, and parsing through more data – data that was *way* out of my league. Talk about your scientific jargon; the research quickly moved from something I could easily interpret to something that was practically a foreign language to me.

There wasn't any info attached to my photo, aside from code and science jargon. Even if I had looked up each word, I doubt I would have understood it.

The burning thought that remained at the back of my head was the fact that this research project had a photo of me.

"Relax, Writer Gideon."

"This, I ..."

"It is a lot of information, but relax for now. Your thoughts are too fast."

"You can read my thoughts, that's right. Grace."

She looked down at me, her eyes slowly morphing from white to blue.

"Yes?"

"Why is my picture in here? I know why you're here; I mean, I know why your picture would be in here, but why is my picture in here?"

She sniffed, and a tear began to fall down her cheek.

"Writer Gideon."

"Please, Grace, tell me something. Just put these pieces together for me, and then we can figure out what the next step is."

Was I a test subject?

God, that sounded stupid to think.

I'd lived just about as normal a life as an American could live. I'd never been abroad, never been in trouble with the law, never had a speeding ticket. I had a degree from a state university and paid my taxes on time every year. Surely that shit counted for something.

"Please shut down the computer," she said. "I want to go outside."

"Outside?" I considered it for a moment. No one seemed to be after us just yet. That didn't mean there wouldn't be someone after us in the near future, but I figured it couldn't hurt to get some fresh air. Especially because we were going to be spending at least a night or two in this hotel, considering all the data I had to comb through.

"Sure, let's go outside for a little bit. I think we can walk to the beach from here. It's not much to look at, but it's not too bad."

"And for dinner?"

"Are you hungry again?"

"No."

I smiled at the strange woman. I had no idea what to make of her – still don't. I looked away once she started to change her form into mine.

"Remember, no shifting in public."

Chapter Eight: The Second Cherry Blossom Girl

I'm not going to bore you with the story about how we went to the beach, and how we sat there for a while watching the waves lash against the shore, or how some seagulls flew by squawking and fighting over a bit of garbage, or how the sun started to set and it was gorgeous.

As Luke would say, *action, action, action,* and boy, would this turn out to be the basis of my evening once we got back to the hotel.

Grace and I had both just gotten into bed when I heard something crash down the hall. I didn't really think much of it … until the door handle shot across the room as if it had been loaded into a gun and fired.

The door flew off its hinges and crashed into the window on the far wall, shattering the glass and letting in a cold gush of air.

That was when I found out there was another cherry blossom girl, and she wasn't happy.

I recognized her immediately; she'd been in one of the pictures I'd discovered on what I was now calling Grace's drive.

The woman resembled Grace. She could have even been a sister.

She was tall, with short blonde hair, a light complexion, and a predatory face. She wore a tight black bodysuit that accentuated her curves as she stalked toward us. But before she could get any closer, she suddenly fell sideways and cracked her head against the wall.

My blood was pulsing, the ability to move obsolete, and my heart thundered in my chest as Grace turned to me, her eyes blaring white.

"Who is she?" I asked, barely able to get the words out.

Grace was breathing hard as well. She sat now in her original form, still wearing the clothes I'd given her back in my basement apartment.

"She's like me."

I had already determined that, but the confirmation helped me come to grips with what had just happened. I had just seen the door handle spear across the room and the door itself fly off its hinges. Of course she was just like Grace, but I had no idea what type of power she possessed or who else was after us.

This was on my mind as I finally scrambled to my feet and started packing. It was instinctive at this point: run, run, run.

If anything, I needed to bring my laptop and its charger; I needed to be able to plug back into Grace and figure out what was going on and why I was somehow a part of it.

I hadn't forgotten about my picture, but I'd been too distracted by the beautiful woman and the beach over the last few hours to investigate further.

"We're out," I told Grace. *"Now."*

"She killed three people."

If my life were a movie, this would be the scene in which they play some ironic 1970s psychedelic tune while they panned the camera over my confused, befuddled, half-afraid, and utterly colorless face, as I realized just what I'd gotten myself into and tried to come to grips with what I was about to do.

"Writer Gideon, did you hear me? She killed two of the security guards and the receptionist." She changed into the black woman at the front desk. "This one," she said before she shifted back.

"The hotel had security guards?"

I didn't remember seeing any muscle in the lobby. I didn't remember seeing anyone, really, aside from a trucker, and a couple with an SUV. And the only reason I'd seen their SUV was because they pulled up in it while we are walking back from the beach.

"No, the same men from the cherry blossoms," she said. "The same type of men."

Her hands trembled, and I wanted to throw mine out and grab hers and tell her it was going to be okay.

Only I didn't know if it was going to be okay.

I was in way over my head, and it was only one day later, just about twenty-four hours since she arrived naked on my doorstep. I had no idea what was in store for me, but if it resembled what had just happened, *we were fucked.*

"Your mind is wild again, Writer Gideon."

I clapped my hands together. "Sorry, just getting a lid on this. So, we taking her or not?"

Grace bit her lip.

"She's like Magneto or something," I said aloud, pacing before the bed. Needing to do something with my hands, I checked my duffle bag again and slung it over my shoulder.

"Magneto?" Grace's eyes flashed as my thoughts became hers.

"Well?"

"Not exactly, but there are some similarities."

"Okay that's fine, but I really need to know if we're bringing her with us, or if we're just trying to get the hell out of here. I probably shouldn't even order a vehicle – I probably should just …" I glanced at Grace. "We need to steal a car."

"Okay," she said, her eyes still white. "We can steal the SUV that belongs to the couple we saw earlier."

"I may have to put a moratorium on reading my mind ..."

She smiled at me. "Sorry, bad habit."

"Let's just get out of here." I stopped in front of the other woman. She didn't look very heavy, so I decided to try to lift her over my shoulder. Once I did so, I felt my energy dissipate from my body.

My knees started to buckle, but before I could fall completely, Grace placed her hand on the woman's head and the feeling subsided.

"What was that?" I asked, my energy returning as I hoisted the other woman over my shoulder.

"It was her. She is like ..." Grace paused for a moment as we entered the hallway, her eyes narrowing as she thought of a way to describe it. "She drains your life."

"A vampire?"

She gave me a funny look. "Those aren't real."

"Sorry, I just figured ... well, I have a psychic shifter with me, why not add a vampire? Also, I just finished reading a vampire novel by George R.R. Martin called *Fevre Dream.* A lot of people don't know that he wrote a vampire novel. Sorry, thinking out loud."

I recalled the book and one of its protagonists, a vampire named Joshua York, the Pale King, the bloodmaster.

"This isn't a book, and we should probably go."

"Right," I said as we exited the room.

We stopped in front of the elevator, the woman still flung over my shoulder and Grace next to me, now holding my duffle bag.

It was when we got to the lobby that I realized how fucked we truly were.

The receptionist had been impaled by a lamp, still in her chair. To my left, one of the paramilitary soldiers – still had no idea what to call them at that point – was in a fetal position, completely shriveled up and as red as a strawberry. The other was in two pieces, his body demarcated by a steel slab that had been ripped from the wall.

This was the one that caused me to vomit. To my credit, I vomited while still holding the woman over my shoulder, which must count for something. But vomit I did, my throat stinging of acid and oily pizza.

"Sorry," I gasped as I took in the scene for a second time. I had the notion of leaving the vampiric Magneto woman behind, but something told me she'd be worth more with us rather than against us.

Of course, Grace sensed this. "She's a bit more trouble than me."

"I didn't think that was possible," I said, staggering a bit.

A dozen thoughts hit me at once, all centering around what to do with the bodies.

"We can't just leave them here," I said as I set the woman down on a sofa. Later, of course, I would have just left them. But at the time I still thought cleaning up the bodies would be the right thing to do.

"They're not our bodies," Grace said coldly.

"Yeah, I can see that, Grace, but if we leave them here and more people see this, we're doubly screwed, because local law enforcement will get involved."

"So, what should we do with them?" she asked, placing her hands on her hips. She looked cute in the moment – a thought that made me feel guilty, especially with the carnage all around.

"I can't believe I'm saying this …" I shook my head and just let it out. "We need to go to that couple's room, get the keys to their SUV, load the bodies in the back, and figure out how to get rid of them. We need to do it quickly, as quickly as humanly possible."

Grace shrugged. "Okay."

"Seriously? That's your reply to what I just said?"

She nodded. "They're in room 106. Should we go now?"

"Yeah, will she be okay?" I tilted my head toward the other superpowered woman.

"She's going to be like that a while."

I swear Chinua Achebe whispered in my ear at that exact moment. "If we put ourselves between God and his victim, we may receive blows intended for the offender," he wrote in *Things Fall Apart*.

If ever there was a book title that described where my life had come …

I sighed. "Let's get the bodies."

Chapter Nine: Getting Rid of Dead Bodies Ain't Easy

It was relatively easy to get the keys to the SUV.

Basically, Grace just knocked on the door and asked for it. Of course, she'd morphed into their daughter or something to make it more convincing, not that she needed to do that because of her psychic abilities.

The doting father came running back with the keys, and we had transportation.

Had I been given the chance to do it again, I would have instructed Grace to tell the couple to load the bodies for us. But these kinds of ideas would come later, after I'd grown used to being with a psychic.

We needed to hurry.

It wouldn't be long before someone came and called the police. To run interference just in case, Grace stayed in the lobby while I went outside, got the SUV, and drove it up to the check-in lane.

I popped open the back of the SUV and ran back inside.

It's hard to believe I'm telling someone this, but the first thing I did was take the bottom half of the severed body. It was surprisingly heavy, and as I carried it, I started to dry heave.

I was able to keep it down this time and steeled myself as I went back to get the rest of the body. His torso was much heavier, and I was glad he wore a black helmet with green lights on it that prevented me from seeing his face. His entrails though ... there are some memories I'd like to forget, and that is definitely one of them.

I made a bloody mess of getting him to the vehicle, which I realized only made this crime scene more damning. Too late to do anything now, and I wasn't about to leave any bodies behind. At least the fact that there were no bodies along with the bloodstains and signs of violence threw a loop in whatever police procedure would follow.

I would have hated to be the detective tasked with figuring out what went on here. Which reminded me. Before I got the second body, I went into the office and saw a small box with cables feeding into it. The box was hooked to a television that showed four video images from the front desk area and the check-in lane.

I unplugged everything.

Realizing that wouldn't do shit, I opened the box and pulled out the hard drive. I dropped the hard drive on the ground and stomped it.

What are you doing? I thought as I picked up the now-dented hard drive and held onto it. I'd seen enough TV to know the cops could CSI the shit out of even a broken one.

Panic had taken over by this point. I quickly ran back out to the SUV, threw the drive inside – I could deal with it later – then returned to the lobby.

I dragged the second body to the vehicle. This one was a little lighter due to the fact that the guy's skin had shriveled up. I didn't know what vampiric Magneto did to him, but it was absolutely terrifying, and I hoped I would never be on the receiving end of her special abilities.

Finally, I took the receptionist, who I placed on top of the others. This one was the hardest – I had actually interacted with her and she didn't deserve to die – and just seeing her hair spill over when I set her on top made me hate myself.

"You are an accomplice to murder," I whispered as I went back inside to grab Grace and the other superpowered woman.

By this point, my back was screaming at me, and my calves hurt. I wasn't used to carrying anything, let alone actual people. So, I was glad to finally place the other woman in the back and cover the bodies with a tarp. I set my duffle bag on top of them and got in the SUV. Grace climbed in on the other side.

Even though it was chilly out, I'd worked up a sweat. I knew I was an idiot for leaving blood stains in the lobby, but I didn't have time to mop. This gave me an idea, a fucking brilliant idea.

"Follow me," I told Grace.

We got out of the SUV and returned to the receptionist area. Sure enough, there was number on the phone for the maid staff; they apparently had a room in some other part of the complex. We called them, and an older white lady appeared a few excruciatingly long minutes later.

She immediately went into a trance when she locked eyes with Grace.

"Sure, I'll clean all this up," she said, "and I won't remember any of it."

"Easy enough," I said as we returned to the SUV. Grace got in the front beside me, and I started the vehicle up.

I held my breath for a moment, afraid I'd smell the bodies. Once I couldn't hold it any longer, I inhaled deeply through my nose and realized I couldn't smell anything. At all. Damn sinuses.

After navigating the neighborhood for a moment, we did the loop around and I pulled into the parking lot of a Home Depot. I got my phone out as Grace read my thoughts and relaxed.

"Just texting a friend," I told her. "And please, make sure the other one doesn't wake up. Does she have a name, by the way?"

"Yes. It's Veronique."

I looked at her curiously for a moment. "So you know *her* name, but you don't know your own?"

She turned and looked out the window at a man rolling some wooden slabs to his truck.

"Okay, we'll deal with that later."

I pulled up GoogleFace messenger and click on Luke's icon.

Me: Hey, got a minute?

Luke: What's up?

Me: So, I've run into a little issue in my story and I wanted to pick your brain.

Luke: Lay it on me.

Me: My main character and the shifter were at a hotel, when this other superpowered woman kicks the door down.

Luke: Did you just introduce a harem?

Me: I hadn't even thought of that, but let's work through my issue first: there are three dead bodies in the hotel, and my MC wants to get rid of them.

Luke: Why does he want to get rid of them? I mean, why does he care if they are there or not?

Me: Well, he already knows the government is probably after him, but he doesn't want to get local law enforcement involved. Because then it would create like a lot of things he doesn't want to have to deal with, and that I don't want to have to deal with as a writer, you know, police procedural things, etc. He'd rather skip all that and get back to the story.

Luke: Aah, I see. That stuff is tedious, and if you get it wrong, someone will inevitably leave a review about it. Okay, so he has three bodies.

Me: One of the bodies is cut in half, but yeah, he has three. And he has an SUV, that he stole, or that the psychic shifter stole from a couple in the hotel. Right now, I have him with the three bodies in the back of the SUV and he's parked in front of a home improvement store.

Luke: I see. Okay, how about this: he takes them to the nearest dumpster and drops them in.

Me: That could work.

Luke: Wait, what happened to the other woman, the one who kicked down the door? She has superpowers, right?

Me: She's in the SUV too, passed out in the back seat. She has vampiric Magneto abilities. The psychic woman, who I'm calling Grace, put her ass to sleep.

Luke: Okay, I really like where this is going. So you have ...

Me: I don't have, my main character has.

Luke: Lol. Okay, your MC has an SUV full of dead bodies, and you need to get rid of said bodies.

Me: Yep.

Luke: And where is the setting for the story, are you like in a big city, or you near the ocean?

Me: The story is set near the ocean, or at least a big body of water, and I'm talking really big here, like the Great Lakes.

Luke: Is there any cement around?

I glanced up at the Home Depot. The last letter on their bright orange sign flickered. Above and to the left of the building, a half moon hung in the sky, its bottom portion covered by a single black cloud.

Me: There could be some cement around. Like I said, they are in the parking lot of a home improvement store.

Luke: You could cement their feet and toss them in the ocean.

Me: The only problem with that is that he doesn't have a lot of time. And he also doesn't want to be traveling around with the bodies in the car.

Luke: That's understandable, it'd be a pain in the ass to deal with some dead bodies in the car; I hope you didn't write yourself into a box.

Me: A box? No. There must be some way.

Luke: I got an idea! You said you could get another car, right? I mean you can have the psychic do just about anything, so you should

be able to get another car. Just get another car and leave the bodies in
the SUV. Let law enforcement sort it out off scene.

Me: Yeah, I didn't think of that, maybe I could leave the SUV and
trade it out for another car.

Luke: That could definitely work, especially if you leave the SUV
somewhere where the cops won't find it for a bit. Maybe have the MC
drive it to a secluded location. At least long enough for your readers to
forget about that and move on to the next bit of action. Remember:
action, action, action.

Me: You've saved my life yet again, buddy – thanks.

Luke: No problem, let me know if you run into any other plot holes.
This is a pretty crazy story you got going here.

Me: It is definitely shaping up to be something unique.

I turned to Grace and smiled. "Ready to steal another car?"

It was cold out, a frigid wind whipping against our faces. A few
seagulls had taken refuge in the parking lot, gathering under a
lamppost.

"Hello," Grace told the couple with the convertible BMW with
halogen lights. They had just pulled into the Home Depot parking lot

and were in the process of getting out of their vehicle when we approached.

She had taken on the appearance of a Hispanic woman, her hair long, dark, and flowing, her skin caramel, and her clothing tight.

She'd borrowed the body from a woman who sold fiber tablets and other weight loss products. I'd seen the actress on a dozen infomercials, that smile of hers utterly contagious.

"Can we help you?" the owner of the BMW asked.

He was a fifty-something-year-old white man with a splattering of gray hair, a soul patch, and a light green sweater vest. His wife was similarly dressed.

I stood next to her, my hat low so the brim partially concealed my face. "Remember what I told you," I said to Grace under my breath.

Her eyes flashed white. "We need your car."

"My car?"

I glanced between the two, tension rising in my chest.

"Sure, sounds like a good idea to me. We'll give you the car." The man reached into his pocket for his keys. He looked at his wife and she nodded, a blank look on her face.

"You will take this SUV to …" Grace hesitated.

"California," I said.

"You will take this SUV to California. Once you're in California, you will leave the SUV at a ..."

"WalMacy's."

"You will leave the SUV at a WalMacy's in California," she said softly. "Then, you will come back to Connecticut, where you will forget about all of this."

I cleared my throat. "The bodies in the back ..."

"Yes," she said as she focused on the couple. "You will not look at the bodies in the back of the vehicle. You won't even think about the bodies or anything else in the back."

"Not a problem. We'll just hurry and drive to California." The guy told his wife as he handed Grace the keys.

"The hard drive ..." I whispered to her.

"And there is a hard drive in the SUV. Please get rid of this on your way." She looked at me. "How should they get rid of it?"

"Throw it off a mountain, drown it, smash it to pieces, doesn't matter."

"Sure, you got it, doesn't matter. We'll handle it," the man said.

And with that, we had a new ride.

I kept waiting for her abilities to falter, to not take effect. This only made me think of what we could possibly do once we figured out what was going on, and once I got better at working with her to manipulate people.

The sky was the limit at that point.

I checked over my shoulder to make sure there were no other cars in the parking lot, and once I saw that the coast was clear, I walked to the SUV and lifted Veronique out of the back.

She was still out cold, and as I set her into the back seat of the convertible BMW, I made sure to buckle her up. Safety first! I waved to the couple as they got in the SUV and the man in the sweater vest waved back.

"Where are we going now?" Grace asked as she got into the BMW beside me. Her face melted away and she was back to blonde hair and Norwegian features.

"We need to get out of New Haven, so …" I thought for a moment. "Let's go to Stamford for the night. There are a ton of nice hotels downtown, and it should be an easy place to hide."

"Can we see the cherry blossoms again before we go?" she asked suddenly, a softness creeping into her Arctic blue eyes.

"As long as you don't mind seeing them at night," I said as I started the beamer.

"No, that's okay."

My phone buzzed as I pulled onto the highway. After a quick glance, I saw it was one of my co-workers, a guy named Dave. He was wondering if I could come in early tomorrow to cover his shift.

Nope.

I deleted the message.

It was still hard for me to imagine that so much about my life had changed in such little time.

If Grace hadn't shown up, I would have gone in to work for Dave and just continued my humble, yet quite frankly, boring existence in New Haven.

I would have continued to work at the Yale gift shop that also sold lamps. And I would have been working tirelessly on *Breakpoint Online*, a book that had already been written so many times in similar ways that no one would have given a shit about it.

"Focus on the road, Writer Gideon," Grace said.

"Will do." I gripped the steering wheel, smiling at its sleek leather texture and the way it felt in my hands. The BMW's dashboard was lit up like a cyberpunk carnival, yet it was still minimal, avant-garde even.

"Roof down?" I asked Grace.

She glanced up at the roof and nodded. "We can see the stars if the roof is down."

"For sure. We'll bring it down once the coast is clear."

It only took us about five minutes to get to Wooster Square. Once we slowed, I pulled the beamer in front of an Italian bakery and checked the center console for the convertible button. I assumed it was the button with the arrows surrounding the roof and pointing downwards.

Bingo.

"This is going to be cool," I told her. "Trust me." The mechanized roof whirred as it settled into the back. "Also, you should probably change forms real quick."

"To what?"

If you're thinking that I hadn't really thought this through, *you're right.*

Here I was, riding around in a convertible BMW with the top down and a dangerous woman passed out in the backseat, not to mention the woman who had escaped some secret lab in the passenger seat, her blonde hair and features a beacon if there ever was one.

"Let's make this quick," I told Grace as I turned my blinker on. "And change into anything you want, aside from me or my mom."

Grace changed into the male newscaster from earlier, a crisp blue suit, pocket square, and tie clip forming as her shoulders lengthened and her chest pulled taut.

"How about a female version of that?"

Her body shrank as she turned into the geisha wearing the newscaster's suit.

"Happy?"

"Better, but lose the geisha hair and ease up on the makeup. Remember, we don't want to draw attention to ourselves."

Her hair relaxed, and the white makeup disappeared. Now she looked like an Asian woman in her significant other's suit.

"Cool," I said as I pulled the beamer back onto the street.

Damn, it feels good to be a gangster, I thought as I moved slowly around the square so Grace could see the cherry blossoms. I wasn't quite a badass yet, Walter White's son to Walter White proper, but I could at least say that I'd seen some shit.

And no, I still wasn't worthy of getting a tear tattoo on my face, but hell, it had only been a day and I had already handled dead bodies – something that would be hard to stomach if I actually sat around and thought about it.

Still, not quite time for a tear tattoo.

I saw the entrance to my basement apartment a couple blocks away and felt the urge to stop in and check the place.

That, of course, would be the noobest of noob moves, so I just continued along.

I circled the block twice, enough times to get a whiff of the cherry blossoms.

Damn if they weren't pretty, even at night.

Like floating cotton balls on the surface of a dark body of water, the blossoms were as intriguing as they were fleeting, gone in a short amount of time only to reappear again.

Passages like the last one were the reason I never attempted to write romance or literary fiction.

Feeling the chill in the air, and worried that someone would see us, I pressed the button on the center console that brought the top back over our heads.

Grace turned to me and I watched as her Asian features vanished. She was herself again, Lady of Lorien cosplayed by a buxom porn star.

She locked eyes with me and her clothing started to morph. She was now in a tight red dress, something Jessica Rabbit would barely fit into.

"Too skimpy for Stamford, Connecticut," I told her with a laugh.

She playfully snapped her fingers and she was in black latex, the zipper over her chest unzipped all the way to her belly button.

It was then that I realized she was reading my mind, going through the images in my head …

Her form changed again, and she wore a fishnet body stocking, latex boots, and cat ears.

I gulped as I realized she'd found my personal spank bank.

"Ha! Not that one, just, um, regular clothes while I'm driving," I said, distracted as hell. Luckily, Highway 95 wasn't too crazy. There were a few eighteen-wheelers, and the occasional granny driver, but traffic was moving along at a good clip.

"You sure?" she asked, still in the fishnet getup and cat ears.

"Yes, and please, don't read my mind, especially not there."

"Don't turn into your mom and don't read your mind," she said. Her clothing faded into the clothing I'd given her back at my apartment. "Better?"

I nodded as a car with bright lights pulled behind me.

The car eventually swerved around, and I had the notion to tell Grace to zap the driver with some bad nightmare juju, but I behaved myself, remembering that I was now a fugitive and had committed some type of felony by moving the bodies.

Better to keep a low profile and not cause a highway accident to appease my road rage.

An idea came to me as the BMW purred along the highway. I connected my phone's Bluetooth to the radio, scrolled to my podcast app, and played the first one my finger landed on.

"Can you make your voice sound like his?" I asked, as Ira Glass gave his *This American Life* intro.

Grace cocked her head to the right as she listened to the voice. Finally, she nodded, and as I turned the radio down, she began speaking in his famous voice.

"Hi, Writer Gideon, I am talking to you as the man on the radio. Each week I talk to you as the man on the radio. What else do you want me to say?"

I snickered. "Say anything."

"Anything."

"You know what I mean. Okay, fine, let me ask you some questions. Who is the woman in the back seat?"

"That's Veronique," she said in Ira Glass's distinct voice. "She's like me, but different."

"I remember you telling me something like that. And what are her powers?" I slowed my speed to get behind a white SUV. I should have put the vehicle on auto drive, but I felt like being in control at the moment.

"Like I told you, she can do things with metal, and she's like a vampire."

"And she has the plug on her neck too? I was meaning to check but ... well, the last hour has been pretty crazy."

106

"She has the same port," Grace said in Ira Glass's voice.

"Good. We can look around once we get to our hotel. Let's stay at a nice place tonight – high up, expensive, exclusive. What do you think?"

I glanced at her. The lights of the highway lamps cast diagonal arcs across her face.

"Sounds good to me," she said in her own voice.

Chapter Ten: Snuff Videos

Stamford had a pretty sick downtown for a less-than-large city. There were skyscrapers and a ton of expensive condos, mostly owned by people who took the train into Manhattan. WWE had their headquarters there, and as we took the exit to the city center, I saw their flag flying on the right side of the highway.

I wondered if Vince McMahon was there now, plotting his next attempt to make the XFL viable.

Once we arrived in the city, I located the Marriott downtown. We were going to stay in style this time.

"Same plan as before," I told Grace. "Except this time, we need to bring a body in with us."

"Veronique."

"Yep." I nodded my head over my shoulder. "I need you to make sure everyone we see just thinks she's sleeping and that I'm carrying her. No – better, she's drunk. Make anyone that looks at us think she's drunk."

"Drunk?" she tilted her head slightly.

"It's what happens when you drink too much alcohol."

"I see."

I thought about Veronique's current getup. She wore a tight black mil-spec suit with molded armor on almost every part of the suit. It was the closest to an actual supervillain outfit I'd seen.

"What are you getting yourself into?" I whispered as the concierge approached my car. I handed him the keys as we got out of the vehicle.

"She's drunk," I lifted Veronique into my arms. "Who knew the, um, wells were so strong here in Stamford?"

The concierge, a young, Indian guy, glanced from Grace, who also wore a tight black outfit, back to Veronique. He nodded at me as he put two and two together and got threesome.

"It's not what it looks like," I said. "Grace, wipe his mind after this."

He started to say something but suddenly, his face went blank.

I turned to Grace and caught her eyes going from white to blue. Without asking, she got my duffle bag out of the trunk and we entered the lobby.

The place was posh; the ceilings were high, the seating ample, and to the left, a fifteen-foot-long glass panel had been erected before a flickering fire. The hotel clerk greeted us, and after a few formalities, she said our executive suite on the top floor was ready.

She handed us our room keycard, smiled thinly, and told us to enjoy our stay.

"How did you know I wanted the penthouse?" I asked Grace as we approached the elevator.

Mind reader, I reminded myself.

You are right, she said in my head.

"You know what? Fine, you can read my mind sometimes, but no talking in my head."

"Too many voices there already?"

"Exactly."

The elevator took us to the top floor and after a quick trip down a long hallway, we entered our room.

Of course I gasped.

About the best hotel I'd stayed at up to this point was a Holiday Inn. This was something else entirely.

The executive suite had two rooms, a kitchen, a balcony with a view of the city, and enough glitz and glam to give Gatsby a hard-on. There were paintings on the wall, slick wood accents, an abundance of space, a seventy-inch wall-mounted television, and cashmere throws on the two sofa chairs.

"Holy shit," I mumbled as I took in the room, nearly dropping Veronique. "Where should I set her?"

"In the second room. The big bed is for us."

Don't have to ask me twice, I thought as I moved her to the second room. Running lights on the floor lit up as I entered. This room was decorated in a similar way to the first, with a small table in the corner.

I placed Veronique on the bed, black combat boots and all, and asked if there was anything else I should do for her.

Grace shrugged. She stood in the doorway watching, an indecipherable look on her face.

"How much longer until she wakes up?" I asked. "And do you think I can plug in while she's asleep?"

"Sure. If she wakes up while you're checking her, I'll shut her down."

A cold chill moved through me as I considered the way she'd said this.

Shut her down?

"You two aren't androids, are you?" I asked, still not convinced that they were entirely human.

She smirked. "You already asked me that, and no."

"If she wakes up, will she try to kill us?"

Grace considered this for a moment as I set my laptop up on Veronique's bed. "Maybe," she finally said.

After the long day I'd had, I was definitely interested in crawling up into that king-sized bed next to Grace. I tried not to think this, though, all too aware that she'd know any thoughts I had.

I booted up my laptop, found the port on Veronique's neck, removed the fleshy covering and plugged in.

In the process, I finally got a chance to get a better look at Veronique.

Her hair was much shorter than Grace's, cut in a bob, and her features more pronounced, sharper and harder around the edges. She was lean and muscular, her torso long, and even though she was lying down, she still seemed poised to strike. Seriously, whatever mad scientist designed these two gene-therapy wonder women was one horny bastard.

I plugged in and the login screen popped up.

"Password?"

"Same as mine," Grace said. "Username: 1351885. Password: 1QAZ2WSX3EFV4321QWEASD."

"Please write that down for me."

She returned a moment later with the information written on the hotel pad. I keyed in the username and password and a new shadow box appeared, similar to Grace's, with a series of dropdown folders.

Veronique's drive was much easier to navigate. I checked her deets and quickly moved on.

Veronique, Subject V.

Build: 2.7341

Base height: 171 Centimeters

Base weight: 50 kilos

"Hello, nurse," I said as I discovered that she had actual stats.

The gamer fiction writer in me rejoiced.

The six base stats had an adjustable dial next to them. Clicking and turning it to the right caused the other dials to adjust accordingly.

A digital number over each base stat made it easy to adjust. Again, if I adjusted one, it adjusted them all, and they could only be adjusted up to the number ten, making min-maxing easy as hell to do.

I settled on some numbers I was comfortable with:

Strength: 4

Intelligence: 6

Constitution: 7

Wisdom: 5

Dexterity: 6

Charisma: 2

She wasn't very strong, and she had the charisma of a pet rock, but she would be smart. And besides, most of her abilities lied about her superpowers.

Or magic. I still wasn't sure what I should call this shit.

"Superpowers sounds cooler," Grace said, her eyes slightly white, her pupils little black dots.

"Works for me."

I drilled down further in the abilities menu to figure out exactly what Veronique could do. Unfortunately, there wasn't anything I could modify in here, at least not yet.

Aside from base information, everything else was grayed out. Still, there was enough for me to get a handle on her powers and what she was capable of.

Frightening stuff, too – especially her 'vampire-like' ability to drain a person's life. I recalled the shriveled security goon back at the hotel and the fact that she'd started to do the same to me until Grace knocked her out.

I gasped as I saw a series of test videos.

"Do I really want to click this?" I asked aloud.

Grace nodded, and I figured it couldn't hurt.

If we were going for the Pandora's Box analogy, I would have already ripped the lid off, thrown it across the room, and pissed in the box.

In the last twenty-four hours I'd seen dead bodies, had my mind read by a shifter, stolen two vehicles, become a fugitive, and watched another superpowered woman blow the handle off a door (still hadn't explored *that* power yet).

So if it was a snuff video, I was ready.

"Fuck yes, I want to see this." I clicked on the first video.

Sure enough, it was a snuff video.

In the clip, a blindfolded inmate handcuffed to a handicap chair was rolled into a room. His shirt was removed, and the only reason I assumed he was an inmate was his jumpsuit and the number written across his chest in permanent marker.

A younger Veronique wearing a blue hospital gown approached him with her hand raised.

With an indecipherable look on her face, she touched his arm and it began to shrivel.

As it did, her own skin tone and luster started to change. I stopped the video there and started it again from the beginning, realizing this time that she looked slightly emaciated at the start. Toward the end, she looked absolutely vibrant.

She feeds off people's energy?

I played the clip back.

As she pressed her hand into his arm, his skin turned the color of beef jerky. A red aura appeared above her tiny fingers as the plague quickly covered his entire body. He died, his face purple, his eyes rolled into the back of his head, his muscles mangled.

Veronique turned to the camera and smiled faintly.

"Well, that was fucked up." Naturally, I clicked another video. I mean, who wouldn't by that point?

The next video was of her doing the same thing to an animal. They had a lamb chained up in a room – how sacrificial! – and as soon as she touched it, someone's future dinner and/or wool coat shriveled up and fell to the side.

She started crying after killing this one.

"So, she can suck the life force out of an animal …"

Grace nodded, her eyes still white. This was the longest I'd seen them remain this color.

"Well, at least she likes animals."

Nope, not even that fact made what she was doing okay. I also found it odd that she'd cry after the animal and not the human.

But she isn't the one doing this stuff, I reminded myself. *I mean, she is, but she's being told to do it. They are telling her to do it.*

Cue the *Stranger Things* theme.

I clicked another video. She was older in this one, her curves starting to take shape beneath her hospital gown. There were two inmates chained to chairs, back to back, with their shirts off.

Numbers were written on their chests, and one was clearly a skinhead with his swastika, Pepe the Frog, iron cross, and straight up Hitler tattoo.

As if she knew who the former German dictator was – which she very well could have – Veronique lightly drummed her fingers against the inmate's shoulder Hitler tattoo. He cried out, and the man tied behind him soon suffered the same fate. The skinhead died first, the other guy not long after.

Tendrils of red energy left Veronique's hand as she pulled it away from the inmate's shoulder.

"What about her other abilities?" I mumbled after watching yet another snuff video.

This one had featured two men in suits next to her, their faces covered by surgical masks. When I observed the two secret agent men nonchalantly watching someone die, I was reminded of a quote from

117

Confederacy of Dunces: "You can always tell employees of the government by the total vacancy which occupies the space where most other people have faces."

Ha!

I clicked back and arrived at another folder. The second option was labeled with the word 'METAL.'

"So, she's not like Magneto," I whispered as I read through a brief description of her powers. "Or, not entirely like him."

> *Enhanced control over metal:* *Subject V has the ability to manipulate the property of any metal she can see or sense. At her current level, there are size limitations as to what she can manipulate, ranging from up to fifteen times her body weight. For items larger than her and out of the range of her abilities, she can focus on smaller portions of the object.*

"Subject V, huh?" I asked.

Grace nodded as I moved to video evidence.

This stuff was badass.

Veronique could basically rearrange, move, and mold the metal in almost any object.

I watched as she waved her hands in the air and created a metallic statue of pots and pans. In one video, she pulled the radiator off the wall and turned it into a spiny snake. In another, she stopped a bullet, and in yet another, she used her ability to levitate a metal table.

Of course, there was another snuff video too.

These fuckers sure liked their snuff videos, and in this one, she stripped the nails from the wall and killed an inmate chained to a chair.

"So, she's like Magneto," I said.

"Sure," said Grace, her eyes still beaming white. "I'm tired now. Shall we rest?"

Chapter Eleven: Hooking up in Stamford

I'm an idiot, but you already knew that.

My smartphone had been on this entire time, and it was once I brushed my teeth and got into bed with Grace that I realized my folly.

I wanted to be able to talk to Luke – my god, did I need some advice – but I also wanted to limit the ability to track me.

So, I did what they do in movies and television dramas: I removed the battery from my phone, walked out onto the balcony, and hurled it to the empty streets below.

Grace laughed. She was, of course, reading my mind again and knew that I was simply replicating something I'd seen that I had no idea was viable or not. But who could blame me?

I was a product of the twenty-first century. Everything was available at my fingertips and much of my 'knowledge' came from movies and long TV series.

"Let's hope that works," she said.

I grinned at her as I got into bed. "Tomorrow, we'll get a prepaid smartphone at Okay Buy and a mini USB to mini USB. Hopefully, I can mod your abilities using my phone."

"Mod my abilities?"

"I was able to with Veronique; I just don't think I found the right subfolder in your files yet."

"Okay." Grace went into the bathroom and returned a few moments later, wearing a robe that I hadn't seen before.

This got me thinking about another thing that was never resolved with Mystique. If she wore a robe and tore it off, what actually happened?

Grace's robe formed into a black, shiny spandex suit with a zipper on the front, similar to what she wore back in the BMW. It was open all the way to her belly button.

"That's an interesting thing to sleep in," I gulped.

Don't fuck this up, I reminded myself.

I'd watched plenty of anime before and I didn't want to be the semi-loser MC who got all nervous around the girls. I'd read some of the harem gamelit stuff too. Unfortunately, I wasn't a badass tiger-faced dude with stacked muscles and rock-hard abs, nor was I a loser that hadn't been laid in a while who didn't know how to handle the women around him.

I was an anomaly.

Scratch that – *I actually was* that last one, which made me a trope.

You're a goddamn trope! the voice in my head screamed.

"Writer Gideon is thinking about sex," Grace said in a coy voice as her clothing morphed.

If you guessed she was back to her birthday suit, you guessed wrong (although that would have been nice).

She wasn't far off though: topless now, wearing a pair of boy shorts.

Without a word, the shifter got into the bed, mumbled about it being cold, and pressed her feet into my body.

If I were writing this book as a fiction, I'd have the bad guys burst in right now to foil the MC's potential for scoring just to be an ass. Luke would have said something about action, and I would have gone for it. Readers would have felt the tension and my disappointment, and I would have propelled them along, no matter how harrowing my tale.

But true life is stranger than fiction, especially when you associate yourself with psychic shifters.

So, what happened next was *a lot* more innocent than I thought it was about to be.

She fell asleep.

Goddamn me to hell in a handbasket full of sticky cum socks.

Never have blue balls struck a man so hard, but that's what happened as I heard her start snoring softly, her feet still pressed into me.

Focus on your writing, I thought, in an effort to cool down. *You didn't know her intentions anyway.*

Rather than go rub one out – I was trying to be above that animalistic instinct – I started plotting my creative nonfiction account of what had happened to me so far.

When you can't get laid, write! I reminded myself as I kicked the blanket off.

Said every loser writer ever?

Maybe.

As if she were reading my mind, and there was a God who was gracious and good and wanted a writer trying to break bad like Yours Truly to get him some, Grace sat up like a damn vampire, her arms crossed over her chest.

I nearly hopped out of bed when I saw her white eyes, but they softened, and seconds later, she was bringing me in for a kiss.

And damn, it was a nice kiss too.

"You were good today, Writer Gideon."

Shit, she could have told me I was a member of the Flat Earth Society and I would have agreed.

Saying that I was putty in her hands was the understatement of the century.

She could be anyone – and I'm not saying she could be anyone in terms of she could be any person, I'm saying that in terms of we could have sex and she could be any person while we have sex.

Talk about the ultimate fantasy. I could have sex with Natalie Johansson, Oprah, the Queen of England …

Okay, maybe not that last one, but that's what was on my mind as she looked at me – and not those women in particular, just the fact that any fantasy I had was possible. Hell, fantasies I never knew I had were possible.

And of course she understood this. She read my thoughts like they were a book with the font set for seniors.

So, I tried a little experiment.

Instead of asking her, I asked her through thought to her to show me her true form. Not the high elf with white blonde hair and straight up Aryan features; no, I wanted to see her real form, who she truly was under all the personas.

I wanted to get down to basics, and tension between us was so high that I figured it was now or never.

Are you sure?

Do it, I thought back.

Layers of skin began to peel back from Grace's face, her hair morphing into various shades, her skin tightening and loosening, her eyes fluttering as they changed colors, her nose and chin elongating as she cycled through dozens of forms she'd taken.

What was left was a thin, emaciated woman, not unlike Veronique in her snuff videos.

Grace's face was covered in zits and acne scars, her hair dark, her eyes black, her nose small, and her voluptuous features nonexistent.

I gasped, and as I did, she immediately reverted to the form that I'd first met: Scandinavian, white blonde hair, blue eyes, and soft features.

"I didn't mean ..." I cleared my throat. "I wasn't offended. You can be that form with me."

Grace laughed softly. "It was a joke, Writer Gideon, I wanted to see how you would respond. This is my true form." She yawned and lay back down. "You should go back to thinking about your writing while I sleep. Tomorrow, you should write all day. I think what you're planning to do is a great idea, and I think there are more like us."

"More like you and me?"

"No, not like me in particular, more like Veronique and me. Superpowereds. I'm sure there are more, but I'm not able to sense them right now. Maybe they're dead. Maybe they're too far away."

"Yeah, I'll get to writing." I swallowed awkwardly. "Um, it's been nice getting to know you."

Yes, I should have kicked myself in the ass for that line, but I felt like an idiot for how I'd acted over the last few minutes, and I had to say something to save face.

"If you want to do this now and get it out of the way, we can," she said in the way that a doctor would relay a diagnosis.

"Do what?"

She raised an eyebrow at me. "Do you want to put your cock in me?"

I gulped, my face turning red. "It's never been presented to me in that way."

Where did she learn these terms? I wondered, still floored by what she'd said.

In your thoughts. The videos you watched, she said inside my head.

"Please don't read my thoughts!" I smoothed my hand over my face. What twenty-five-year-old American male in 2030 *hadn't* seen his fair share of fucked up porn? I mean, there may have been some Amish guys, or some Mormons out in Utah, but even those dudes had multiple wives and by my age, shit, they would have had multiple kids too.

Grace shrugged. "Okay, then we will make it more romantic. Tomorrow night. I will only read your thoughts if you ask me to."

"Promise?"

"I can't promise that," she said with a soft laugh. "But I can try. You've seen a lot of videos of sex."

"Ahem, I'm aware."

"A lot. Must be thousands in your head. They are quite educational."

"And what about Veronique?" I asked, changing the subject.

"She will be asleep until I tell her to wake up." Grace turned away and pressed her ass into me. "Goodnight, Writer Gideon."

But both of us knew that it wasn't going to end there, and that rather than wait till tomorrow night – especially considering who knew what could happen tomorrow – we both came to the silent decision that we'd better finish it now.

So that's what we did.

It only took a second of her ass being pressed into me for our parts to connect. It was natural, there was nothing unnatural about it. I was in my boxers, she wasn't in anything, and things just happened.

She grabbed me by the waist and pushed my member closer to her and …

The penis took on a mind of its own and searched for the warmest place it could find.

My thoughts were immediately silenced.

As soon as I was in, and she was gyrating her hips, my thoughts were but a battered wind chime beating in the distance. I took her from behind, and she stretched her neck back to kiss me.

Sure, I should have been wearing a condom, but what was the worst that could happen? Superhero babies? Who wouldn't want a superhero baby? And what if she had a disease? Well, I had already signed my death warrant by taking her in to begin with.

So, I wasn't worried about protection.

In retrospect, there were a ton of things I would have liked to try, especially with a shifter, but that was not on my mind the first time we went at it.

Don't cum too soon, don't cum too soon.

That was more of my thought process, because Grace was by far the hottest woman I'd ever been with.

Shit, I had to close my eyes so I wouldn't see her because I knew if I could see her, if I could see the flesh of her breasts moving up and down as I pumped from behind, her neck turned to me and her eyes locked on my face, her throat as she breathed, her teeth as she bit her lip … if I saw those things, then that would be it for me.

That would be all she wrote, and I'd make it just about one minute before blowing my load and calling it quits.

So, my goal then became to make it for two minutes.

Best night of my life? Well, take out the dead bodies, and the fact that we were almost killed in Wooster Square, and I'll give you that one.

It was a damn good end of a damn weird day.

Chapter Twelve: Two Days to Write a Book (or Death)

I woke up at the crack of dawn, ready and able to write my magnum opus. I kissed Grace on the cheek, hopped out of bed, secretly gave myself a pat on the back for being such a badass, grabbed my glasses and my laptop, and went down to the lobby so I could tap out some words.

I wouldn't do things that risky in the future, but I was still new at this whole running from the law and hanging out with badass superpowered women thing, so I still made rookie mistakes.

At least I'd thrown my cell phone away.

I made it to the lobby, grabbed some coffee, and sat down at a big wooden table, not at all focused on the breakfast buffet.

I had the urge to talk to Luke, but I knew it was just as early in Canada and that I could tell him of my escapades later – I mean, the escapades of my MC.

I pulled up my manuscript and checked the word count.

Yep, it was still at three thousand words, which meant Charles Dickens' ghost hadn't logged into my computer last night and typed out a few thousand just to help a brother out.

Damn you, Charles Dickens' ghost!

I needed to set a motto for the manuscript I was writing; something I could get behind, something that would inspire me forward.

Kurt Vonnegut would do the trick, as he often did.

I checked a file I kept on quotes I'd saved from books I had read and found a great quote from *Cat's Cradle*: "Anyone unable to understand how a useful religion can be founded on lies will not understand this book either."

The goal was not to alienate readers. The goal was to expose this terrible government experiment that created women like subject V and subject G – although Grace was the name that I had given her and there was no telling what her actual name was.

There was also no telling what she actually looked like. Or what she sounded like. Or what she really thought because she could just be mirroring your own thoughts.

All this was beside the point – I needed a better quote. I found one from good ol' Barbara Taylor Bradford that I'd read in a writers' self-help book: "A novel is a monumental lie that has to have the absolute ring of truth if it's going to succeed."

Fueled by coffee and the rage to succeed at something that I should not be trying to succeed at – I meant creative nonfiction here – my fingers were all action, little pistons pumping the keys as the words flowed freely.

By God, I was a genius. I was a great writer – a much-praised literary enigma!

I was writing a motivational self-help book alongside the founders of *The Secret*; I was in the Chicago meatpacking plants with Upton Sinclair; I was getting nitty gritty in Tokyo with William Gibson; I was inventing elaborate magic systems with Brandon Sanderson while chain-smoking cigarettes on a balcony overlooking a strip club with Charles Bukowski.

I was James Patterson dictating his 853rd airport thriller to his co-writer; I was in France with Fitzgerald getting FUBAR and arguing with Zelda; I was snorting coke from Stephen King's trash can; I was at the airport with J.K. Rowling, as she finally dreamed the Harry Potter series alive.

Quiet, Writer Gideon.

Even though Grace *hadn't* said this, hadn't thought-beamed this down to me from our top floor penthouse, it was much-needed.

In actuality, I was sitting in a hotel alone, typing about my encounter with a psychic shifter while trying to cook up a self-published, creative nonfiction book that I hoped would be a bestseller.

Delusional, right?

I was also researching what would happen once they caught me; they'd bring either the cops or federal law enforcement officials and a list of how many federal crimes I had committed.

Hell, I was even worried about not showing up for my shift at the Yale gift shop later that day.

So, a lot was going on in my brain, some of those thoughts completely delusional, others borderline pathetic.

But after the coffee settled, and after I told myself to chill the fuck out and stop being unrealistic, the words came rapid-fire. It took me about three hours, but I was up to eight thousand words by the time I decided to take my happy writer's ass back up to the hotel room.

My finished manuscript would be about fifty thousand words or so, and then I had to have it edited, but I had a quick editor fond of Adderall who could turn out a manuscript in forty-eight hours.

I didn't yet know how I would pay her without the payment being tracked, but I figured that was what PayPal was for. I also figured I could probably run money some way through some sub-company in Singapore, and then transfer it anonymously to her account.

Or I could just have Grace hypnotize someone and tell them to transfer the money.

Boom, that would work.

"Lucy, I'm home," I said as I opened the door. I found Grace sitting on the bed, the blanket up to her chest as she watched a morning talk show.

"That's not a bad start, Writer Gideon. Maybe you can write another five thousand words today, or more. If you can write more, maybe I can reward you."

I was living the writer's dream – or nightmare, depending on who you asked.

And to keep the narrative going, I needed to get to Okay Buy to pick up a few more weapons for my arsenal.

I never pictured myself as the type of guy who could afford a convertible BMW, let alone drive one.

I must have looked like someone I would have been jealous of just a week ago – top down, beautiful woman in the front – as we zipped over to Okay Buy. I'm sure we turned at least a few heads.

On the agenda: a mini USB to mini USB, and a prepaid smartphone. Grace had gone for her Asian disguise, and I was in my bearded Yale bulldog disguise. Low profile as ever.

We found the cable and went to check out in the smartphone area. Grace worked her magic, and we left the store with both items. Fastest trip to Okay Buy I ever took.

Of course, we triggered the security alarm at the front door, but we were simply waved through; another advantage of having a psychic with you.

As we drove back to the hotel, we listened to some pop radio station Grace had chosen. It was bad music, manufactured to the point that it just seemed stale, but she seemed to enjoy it, so I didn't start up a diatribe of how bad pop music had become in the 2020s.

I couldn't look over at her without thinking about what happened between us last night, so I kept my focus on the road, and the vehicles, both human-driven and AI driven, that pulled in front of me.

Back to the concierge and Grace pulled her typical stunts. Then we told the front desk that we'd be staying an extra night, and to bill our company.

I had come up with that one actually, "Bill our company."

It made things sound so official. I was the CEO, she was the CFO.

Up to the top floor we went, and as soon as we keyed ourselves into our room, we checked on Veronique.

She was gone.

Panic exploded in my chest. I hadn't even had a chance to set down the Okay Buy bag when a hanger came flying out of the closet.

The metal wrapped around Grace's legs, causing her to spill over just as another one flew out, this one tightening around her neck until her face started to turn blue.

"Stop!" I shouted, so petrified I was unable to move.

Grace cycled through forms as the life was choked out of her.

As Grace gasped, Veronique stepped out from behind the bathroom door, quickly moving over to the shifter and crouching down to touch her.

Her hand glowed red for a moment, and Grace's eyes rolled into the back of her head.

I was panicked, grief-stricken, close to vomiting, happy that I hadn't eaten lunch, barely able to move a muscle aside from twitching my knees.

I stabilized myself with a hand on the dresser, the Okay Buy bag dropping to the floor.

"I didn't kill her," Veronique said as she stood. She was still in her tight black combat outfit. Her short blonde hair was in her face, partially covering one of her eyes, and as she stared at me, I found myself no longer able to breathe.

It was definitely a panic attack, and as I tried to catch my breath – which seemed impossible – she slowly moved over to me.

"I ... I ..."

"You do not have long before I kill you," she said, not breaking eye contact with me. "That is, unless you have something to offer me."

"I have a BMW in the garage downstairs, my laptop too – you can have that." I was babbling at this point, my words falling out of my mouth before I could actually think through what I was saying.

She placed her hand on my shoulder, and my knees grew weak, my stomach lurching. Seeing the red energy radiate from her hand caused my lungs to decompress.

I'd seen what she could do in those videos, and I slowly found myself growing drowsy, delirious, which loosened me a little bit.

I felt drunk now, helpless, slushed.

She removed her hand and helped me over to the bed so that I could sit.

"I'll give you whatever you want," I told her, out of breath. "Just tell me what you want."

"Why did you take her?"

I glanced up at her. She stood in front of me, her hands on her hips as she took me in. "Are you serious?" I asked.

No answer; the look on her face told me she was indeed serious – deadly serious.

"Look, Veronique, she showed up at my doorstep, and now I'm here. Fuck." One quick glance over at Grace's fallen body, and I felt a lump in my throat.

"She came to you?"

"That's right, and she showed me what was on her drive. Does that make sense? I don't know how to explain it, but I plugged into her, just like how I plugged into you." I touched the side of my neck. "The port."

"And?"

"My pictures were on there too." My mouth was dry, and I could hardly focus on anything as fear boiled through me.

I felt empty, hollow even. What could it mean? Why were my pictures there? And here I was, stealing, fucking, and going shopping for electronics, when there could be something terrible happening, something deadly – and something that apparently involved me.

Veronique's dark eyes softened. "Suppose I believed you. Why should I let you live?"

I cleared my throat. "Look, I don't have any powers, aside from …" I tried to think of a joke and then realized it was not the time to be joking. "Never mind, I don't have any powers, like I said. But I can do one thing …"

"Oh?" She tilted her head as she looked at me, her eyes still dark and soulless.

"I don't know what was going on back in that laboratory …" I finally made eye contact with her, showing her I meant business. "But whatever it was, it's wrong, and I intend to expose it."

She took a step closer to me, my head now at the height of her waist. I didn't feel like it was an intimate moment though, I felt like she was seconds away from killing me.

"Expose it?" she started to chuckle a little.

"Yeah, I know it sounds crazy, but I just have this feeling that there are more like you out there. I know there are. I mean, I don't have a hundred percent evidence yet, but I feel it in my gut, and I did find a few things searching around on both of your … hard drives? Can we call them hard drives? You two are human, correct? I mean, Grace said you were."

I recalled having sex with Grace – they were definitely human. Well, at least Grace was.

"Grace? How would you expose what they have done to us?" she asked, the look on her face still harsh and cold.

"I'm glad you asked," I said, a little too enthusiastically. "Sorry, I'm just excited about my solution to all this. But I do have a plan: I'm going to write a book."

"A book?" she asked, her eyebrow rising.

"Let me rephrase. I've already started writing a book, and I'm almost ten thousand words in. The book is about this experience and what you two have gone through."

"A book, huh?"

"I know it sounds crazy, but I'm a self-published author. I want to publish a book about all this, and put details out there on the internet where people can contact me anonymously about what's going on. Hopefully, we can expose and uncover more of these experimental laboratories, or whatever – you get my point. What I'm trying to say is this: whatever they did to you, is not right."

She bit her lip.

"Look, Veronique," I said, reaching my hand out to her.

I grabbed her wrist, which was possibly one of the stupidest things I could have done in that situation considering her ability. Much to my surprise, it worked, and the look on her face softened. "What they did to you, and what I am assuming they have done to others, is wrong."

"How do you know what they did to me?"

"I only got a taste by searching through your drive. They had you killing people at, like, the age of thirteen. That's just the start. What I saw is wrong, and I'm guessing that's only the tip of the iceberg. It's wrong, and we should …"

"Destroy them, and destroy the Rose-Lyle facility."

"I was going to say *expose* them, but ..." I nodded. "You called it the Rose-Lyle facility?"

"Yes, that's its name."

"And that's where all this happened? Grace too?"

"Who is Grace?"

"The other one like you, *her*." I nodded my chin toward Grace's fallen body. "Look, maybe you're right, maybe we should destroy them. Maybe we should destroy all of them, but to do so, we need to know about the existence of the other locations. Just imagine this: I put the book out, some people contact us – and sure, there will be some kooks – but we get some actual information on more of these places. First, we destroy yours, then we destroy the next one."

As Veronique looked me over, a quote from Ambrose Bierce's *Cobwebs from an Empty Skull* came to me: "People who wish to throw stones should not live in glass houses; but there ought to be a few in their vicinity."

"How long will it take you to write this book?" she asked, as she turned her wrist around and grabbed my hand.

Fear ballooned inside my chest.

"At least a couple of weeks," I said, my teeth chattering. "I mean, I'm a fifth of the way there now, so I should finish next week or so. Maybe a little sooner, but I still have to get the cover designed, get the book edited, get it ready to be published ..."

Veronique shrugged. "Okay, I'll give you two days."

"You're serious?"

Something flashed in her dark eyes. "If you are indeed a writer, you will finish this book in two days and publish it at that time, if it does not succeed …"

My hand tensed up as she activated her power, a red aura forming around her fingers.

"I got it," I said hurriedly. I whipped my hand away from hers. "Two days."

"I will give you as much information as I can. You can also get information from her." She touched her foot against Grace's shoulder.

"And you promise you won't kill her?"

"No, I don't promise. But I don't think I'll kill her. We need her, don't we?"

I had taken a personal development course at a job I worked at a few years back, a course which focused on the usage of the pronoun 'we.' It came back to me all of a sudden, even though I'd dozed off toward the end.

"Yes, *we* need her. We really need her. We really, really need her. Please don't suck her energy out anymore."

"We will see how your book looks in two days." She took a few steps away from me and crossed her arms over her chest. "Now, get started."

Chapter Thirteen: Creative Nonfiction Gamer Sci-Fi?

It was time to write my ass off. I had heard of Nanowrimo, the competition in which an author challenges themselves to write a book in a month, but I never heard of being threatened by a superpowered woman to write a book in two days.

It was madness, unorthodox, and damn near impossible, to say the least!

So, outlines were out the window.

My hands trembled as I fired up my laptop. As I fretted, Veronique dragged Grace to the other bedroom.

Using a coat hanger, and her ability to warp metal, she created a pair of handcuffs for Grace and also used one of the bath towels – the one that I had no idea what you were supposed to do with – to cover her eyes.

If Grace did wake up, she would be blindfolded, and her hands would be bound together. I briefly recalled wondering how she would go to the restroom, but instead of asking, I pulled up my manuscript, took a deep breath, kissed each finger, and started pecking away at the keys.

I didn't write more than two hundred words before curiosity killed the writer.

"Why did you blindfold her?" I asked as I went to the second bedroom to find Veronique finishing up. I wanted to make sure Grace was okay, so I asked this question as nonchalantly as possible.

"Her abilities only work if she can see someone. Once she imprints, that person belongs to her."

"But she can tell someone to do something, right?" I asked. "And they will still carry it out if she can't see them, correct?"

"Correct, but her ability to imprint relies on her ability to see someone. This is why she couldn't stop me earlier." She turned to me. "Shouldn't you be writing?"

"Let's go into the other room; I have a few questions I need to ask you to clarify a few things about what I'm writing."

"Don't you want to check her 'hard drive,' as you would say?" she asked, cocking an eyebrow at me.

"Oh," I said, shaking my head. In my mind, 'Check her hard drive' came off as something completely opposite of what Veronique meant. "I checked her yesterday, and I wasn't able to get much info, but I didn't check as deeply as I should have."

"That's something you should do, but if you want to start with me, that's fine." She moved past me. When I didn't follow her right away, she turned back. "Are you coming or not?"

"Tell me everything you know about the experiments that were done to you, where you came from, and who the men were at the hotel," I said after I'd sat down at my laptop. I never thought of myself as an investigative journalist, but if the shoe fit …

A thought came to me.

"Wait, before we get into that, why did you kill the men you came to the hotel with? That's something I can't figure out."

"Maybe I wanted what she wanted." Veronique sat down in a purple armchair and crossed one leg over the other.

Again, ambiguity in the response. I decided to try a different line of questioning: "Okay, let's start here. Who were they?"

With a small sigh, Veronique started up a story that seemed familiar, if it weren't for the fact that it was entirely true. She explained how she had been born in the lab, or at least a lab like it, and the same thing was true for Grace.

She didn't know all the terminology – and hell if I knew – but basically, they were the results of some type of powerful gene editing that allowed them to have their powers, and other people could also have these types of powers, if only their genes could be modified.

The lab where they'd spent a good amount of their life was called the Rose-Lyle Facility, and Veronique and Grace had only physically met once before. Because of Grace's abilities, she was kept in isolation, but Veronique recalled playing with her once, when they were younger.

"How did you know it was her?"

"We have similar features," was her answer.

"What is the ultimate goal of this experiment? Why was it started in the first place?"

She didn't know the exact answer to this, but I didn't need to harken back to a comic written during the Cold War to know that it likely had something to do with building a super soldier.

I remembered thinking at the time how this again felt like a trope, but then, most things in my life felt like a trope.

Veronique was a bit more social than Grace and had gone on the hunt for others before. This was why she was allowed out, whereas Grace had to escape.

With Veronique, they could simply keep her away from people to feed on and she would lose her power. After all, she fed, and was nourished, by touching people and depleting their energy, and her metal-wielding abilities became obsolete if she were placed in a plastic cell, of which they had two of different sizes for when she misbehaved.

"I was always good when we went out. Never out of line."

"Until last night."

She shrugged.

"And who had you gone after before?"

"Others."

I probed more, but that was all I could get out of her.

The usual story of torture – future and past – became evident as Veronique relived some of her experiences. She'd gone through a hell of a lot to become the hardened young woman that sat before me. They'd put her through various psyop drills, from locking her in a small cellar for a week to one occurrence in which they abandoned her in an unknown location and she'd had to get back to civilization.

Which was pretty much a kill-fest.

The reason she'd lashed out became apparent: She was to be phased out, Grace too.

"We were told that they would retire each of us, that the next generation would become the soldiers they wanted." Anger burnt inside her, evident in the way her nostrils flared. "They told us they'd make us fight."

It was an incredible story, but a story that had been told before, played out in comics and movies. I really wished there were a way for me to spice it up a bit, to make it more interesting or a little more original.

But that wasn't the point of creative nonfiction with a sci-fi twist and hints of gamer fiction. And I had a feeling that the more the reader identified with the story archetype, the better it would be received.

Besides all that, *this stuff was true. This had really happened!*

Fuck, I needed to unpack some of this.

"Do you mind if I talk to a friend of mine who's also a writer? I'd like to pitch ideas off him and see what he says."

"You have two days, and if anyone tries to come here, I will kill them and feed off them," she said as if she were ordering a latte at McStarbucks. There was no emotion in her voice; she only wanted the end result.

"Well, he's in Canada, so he won't be able to get here anytime soon. And he's like me."

"Weak?"

"Sure."

"Are all writers weak?"

"Physically, maybe. Mentally, no."

"You are more like the one you call Grace than me. She never had training."

"I've had training, but it's mostly been corporate and related to customer service."

God, I sound like an idiot.

"I went to college," I told her.

"That doesn't matter to me."

"I figured as much."

My thoughts returned to Luke.

He was in Canada, only a few hours away from Connecticut, but still, I wasn't trying to do the 'send two emojis if you're in danger' act by contacting him.

"It'll be a quick conversation, trust me, and then I'll start writing. I have a lot to write in the next two days, and I am not that prolific, nor am I that disciplined, nor am I that fast. You can see now that I'm not that disciplined; I should have started fifteen minutes ago. Point is, I'll make the conversation quick. Sorry for rambling."

To my surprise, she chuckled at this. "I can see why Grace likes you. You think out loud, so she doesn't have to read your thoughts."

"Oh, she reads my thoughts, even though I tell her not to."

To show that she would stop distracting me, Veronique lay on the bed and turned on the television. "Do you mind if I watch?"

"That's fine; I'll just put on my headphones."

Before I did that, I pulled out my unregistered smartphone – registered to some guy who worked at the cell phone area at Okay Buy, courtesy of Grace's ability – and opened up the GoogleFace messenger app.

Me: Luke, I have a problem.

Luke: I wondered when you were going to message me. I was thinking more about your dilemma, and getting rid of the bodies. One thing you could do would be to have the psychic one convince someone that they were alive, kind of like that old movie Weekend at Bernie's, and then they could just put the bodies in their car and drive off.

Me: Actually, I did something similar to that. But that's not my problem now.

Luke: What's up?

Me: So, I'm at a hotel – I mean, my Main Character is at a hotel with the two superpowered women.

Luke: What are their names again?

Me: The good one is Grace, should be easy to remember. She's the psychic. The bad one is Veronique.

Luke: That last one is a French name, and it makes her sound mysterious, which leads the reader to think she shouldn't be trusted.

Me: Very observant, but here's my problem: she has tasked the MC with doing something impossible, otherwise, she'll kill him.

Luke: What happened to Grace?

Me: She was attacked by Veronique and knocked out. Veronique is now asking him to do this impossible thing, or she'll kill him.

Luke: What has she asked him to do?

Me: She wants him to do something that would normally take a couple weeks to a month. That's all I can say about it for now.

Luke: Okay, that's weird of you, but let's roll with it. So, she's asked him to do something that normally takes a bit of time, correct?

Me: Yep.

Luke: Could your MC potentially do it in the time she's given him to do it? I mean, theoretically, like if she had a gun to his head.

Me: I suppose, but it wouldn't be easy, and the final product may not be as good.

Luke: And I'm assuming Grace is still passed out?

Me: That's right.

Luke: And could she potentially wake up within the next two days and do something about Veronique?

Me: Well, I guess, but that's playing with uncertainty.

Luke: Well, you're the writer, and as a writer, you should always play with uncertainty, otherwise it doesn't feel original. Readers like that uncertainty. It keeps them up at night. Have him at least attempt whatever it is Veronique is asking him to do.

Me: Okay.

Luke: And if Grace wakes up, have her kick Veronique's ass.

Me: That brings me to my next issue ...

Luke: Oh boy.

Me: I'm thinking of labeling this as creative nonfiction gamer sci-fi. Does that sound too crazy?

Luke: Yes. How can it be nonfiction if it's also LitRPG and sci-fi? For it to be creative nonfiction, it has to be true, or at least true enough. This stuff isn't actually happening to you, is it?

Me: Of course it is.

Luke: That's a typo, isn't it?

Me: Of course not.

Luke: Lol! Well, I guess that would be a kind of interesting marketing ploy.

Me: Yeah, a marketing ploy, that's what I'm going for. I'm thinking something that blends Vonnegut's Breakfast of Champions, Maugham's A Razor's Edge, Kundera's Immortality, and some stuff written by John Updike. With sci-fi. I realize all this stuff is more literary, but this idea is just so cool. Trust me.

Luke: I trust you. So ... creative nonfiction gamer sci-fi with metafictional undertones? You had me at shifter.

Me: That's for the mainstream audience, the shifter stuff. Who doesn't like a shifter story? Everyone wants a shifter in their life, and who wouldn't trade anything to be a shifter and be able to do whatever they wanted with them? That's straight up deprived fanboy territory. And the superhero stuff, that's cool too. People love superheroes. Besides, there are so many villains in this world.

Luke: True that. There are too many villains.

Chapter Fourteen: Steak and Shrimp with Veronique

I banged on my keyboard for the rest of the afternoon.

As Veronique watched reruns of *Mad Men*, and I felt like a goddamn madman, I tried to put as many words to digital page as humanly possible.

Whenever I came to a point that I didn't know what to do, or how to describe Veronique's backstory, I asked her and she told me what she could. I needed to plug in, but she refused to let me plug into her for the time being, which left Grace.

At about five, I was sixteen thousand words in.

I had written a shitton of words in the last four hours, a lot of them shit, but some of them good. A personal record in any event. My eyes were twitchy, my fingers ached, and my mouth was the Atacama.

I was hungry too, and I didn't have any money to buy food unless I used one of my cards, which I didn't want to do.

But food could wait; I needed more information, and to get it, I needed to access Grace. I used my throwaway smartphone to plug into her neck. Worked like a charm.

Veronique stood near me, curious as to what I would find. With the login details that Grace had given me earlier, I got in and was presented with a shadow box that contained a series of files.

I clicked on the same file I'd clicked on previously and noticed now that there were more options …

It was like reading code or something. I scrolled through thousands of numbers and codes, trying to figure out what they meant and how to interpret them.

I recalled Grace's white eyes as I looked at Veronique's stats.

She had made them more interpretable, which meant that she was even more powerful than I had originally thought she was.

I got to the bottom of the code and found a button that said 'enter.'

When in doubt, press 'enter,' right?

All the Matrix-esque binary mumbo jumbo disappeared and I was left with something akin to Veronique's stats.

Sabine, Subject S.

Build 3.758

Strength: 1

Intelligence: 9

Constitution: 4

Wisdom: 8

Dexterity: 3

Charisma: 6

So, her name is Sabine, I thought, as I scanned her deets.

The cursor changed once I hovered over her name and I realized that I could modify it. One click later and I changed it to *Grace, Subject G*, which sounded like it would have made a great title for a book on finding God and becoming a better Christian.

Also, I wouldn't be able to write that book, especially after the last two days.

Adjusting her stats didn't do much to prevent min-maxing for her intelligence and wisdom, which I wasn't able to adjust down past the number eight.

A few clicks deeper and I found that her psychic abilities also had the same easy to manage dial system.

Unlike before, they also weren't listed as levels.

She played with my mind, I thought as I looked through the options.

Omnikinesis: 1

Second Sight: 1

Psychometry: 5

Telepathy: 8

Clairsentience: 7

Psychokinesis: 1

Hypnosis: 6

I decided not to adjust them for now; I wanted a clear understanding of what they did before I messed with them, and I figured that like her base stats, changing the dial on any of them would fudge up the pre-made build.

Another thing I found interesting when parsing through her stats was that I was able to modify in real time how she appeared.

There were drop-down options for gender, race, skin tone, height, weight, and further options for various body parts. For example, clicking on a face, allowed me to modify her facial features and facial structure in real time, which was really interesting because it created a 3-D map on my smartphone screen that I could adjust with my fingers.

I could pinch her cheeks and mod them, and as I did, a dial in the upper right-hand corner would turn, and her face would actually *morph* in real time.

There was also a toggle button to go back to the form that she started as. I adjusted her cheeks back to their original form and closed the window that allowed me to drill into her shifter abilities.

My stomach rumbled.

"Are you hungry?" Veronique still stood over my shoulder, her shadow looming over me.

"Yeah, some food would be nice, but I can't use my cards to buy anything, and I don't have any cash. Had I known you were going to attack Grace when we came back from the store, I would have tried to get some cash and some snacks ..." I sighed. "Point is, this woman is our only ticket to getting things like food and lodging."

"I wouldn't say she's our only ticket."

"Got a better idea?" I removed the cable from Grace's neck. "And before you suggest it, I'd like *not* to go to another room, kill the people, and steal whatever food they have. Just in case that's what you were thinking: I am not down with murder."

"But you are okay with hiding murdered bodies?" she asked with a crooked grin.

"I'm not going to say I'm a different man now, but I will say that decision was one that had to be made at that point in time."

Not quite a Glomar response, I thought as I ran my hand through my beard, *but not far off.*

"Don't worry, I won't kill anyone without your permission."

"Okay," I said, not at all comfortable with the way she phrased that last sentence. "What are you proposing?"

Veronique turned to the door. "Don't they have a restaurant in this hotel? It looks like a nice expensive hotel, and I'm assuming they have a restaurant."

"Yes, I believe they do."

"Let's just go to the restaurant, order what we want, and I'll take care of the rest. Once we get back to the hotel room, you can continue working on your book."

"Let's see how I feel when I get back. I can at least design a cover tonight. My hands are killing me from typing so much today."

She shrugged. "You still have two days."

"I was afraid you'd say something like that."

I was a man in need of a margarita. So, I ordered one and the most expensive item I could find on the menu, which was some type of steak and shrimp combo. I was ravenous, and I didn't know how we were going to get out of there, so I figured I should eat well.

Besides, Veronique said she was covering the tab. I wasn't sure how, but fuck it, that's where my life was at that moment.

"What do you want?" I asked her after I ordered. Veronique sat across from me, still in her black mil-spec outfit, perusing the menu in the way one would flip through a catalog they weren't at all interested in.

What I wanted to ask was, *Do you actually eat?* I had a sick feeling she was fed inmates rather than real food.

The waiter, a young guy with beard stubble and a mole next to his nostril, looked at us with bloodshot eyes. "Is that it?" He looked like he'd been working too hard, and I totally knew that feeling, which was why I wanted her to hurry up and order.

"None of this food looks good."

"Um, why don't you just order something small then, like a salad?" I asked her.

"A salad? I am a carnivore." She closed the menu and handed it back to the waiter, who looked at her funny, glanced away, and stumbled off toward the kitchen.

I figured now would be as good a time as any to ask her more questions about her life.

"What do you remember from your childhood?" I asked.

"I didn't have a childhood. Mostly training."

"Was there a particular doctor or scientist who led most of the experiments? Do you know anything like that?"

Her face turned white as she bit her lip. Finally, she sighed heavily. "I do know a few things about that, but not much. There was a woman who was there the entire time from the start, at least from what I can remember. But she rarely made contact with us personally, at least me, anyway. Sometimes she observed us from behind glass."

"Was it a one-way glass?"

"When I was a child, no, it wasn't. Then I destroyed it, and we were moved to a new room that had no glass, but the walls were shiny mirrors."

"So, it was one-way. And you saw this woman later?"

"Yes, briefly, when I was going out on a mission. Grace is not the first one who has tried to escape, but most of them never made it past the courtyard, aside from one."

She reached for her water and took a sip from it.

"What happened to that one?"

"We captured him and brought him back."

"So, there are men, or there *were* men, involved in this experiment as well?"

"Only a few, and they were either killed or phased out, aside from the one I mentioned."

"Does he have a name?"

She swallowed hard. "Angel. His name is Angel."

The thought returned to me: *Had I somehow been part of these experiments? Why else would my picture be on Grace's hard drive?* It was a selfish way to insert oneself into a narrative, and truth be told, about the only superpower I had was holding my breath underwater for thirty seconds. But still, something was screwy about all this.

"There must be more like you," I told her. "And as I was saying up in our room, I think getting this book out will help us find them."

"You like to use the word 'us,' don't you?"

"I want to be part of this, and I want you and Grace both to be part of it," I told her quickly. "This will be the most important thing I ever do in my life. If I can expose this, create some change, and stop weird research universities and FCG authorities from creating super soldiers, then I've actually done something with my life."

"Huh."

Veronique was a unique beauty, with a dash of coldness and seductive vampire qualities due to her ability to deplete a person's life force.

I knew there was a better way to phrase and think about what she did rather than 'deplete someone's life force' or 'seductive vampire,' but it was the easiest way for my mind to comprehend it, and I didn't want to get into some mitochondria-depleting-oxygen-reverse-osmosis

163

jargon, or whatever the hell it was she was actually doing when she drained someone's life.

"And what were you doing with your life before?" she asked, bringing my inner monologue to a blinding halt.

"I was working at a Yale gift shop and writing science fiction."

She laughed at this, producing a rare smile on her face just as my margarita came.

A few sips in and my lips and thoughts loosened up. "You forget what you want to remember and you remember what you want to forget," Cormac McCarthy wrote in *The Road.*

If ever there was a theme for my rambling …

Veronique continued sipping her water as I told her about my life – inconsequential details, about who I was and what I'd been up to over the last twenty-five years. She seemed interested though, and I wondered if the blandness of my life had some appeal to the super soldier.

It wasn't long before the steak and shrimp came and with them a side of asparagus and red potatoes that had been baked and fried. The shrimp were juicy and pink, and the steak produced a hint of red liquid around it as I sawed in.

Meat!

My god, was it a good meal, and for a fleeting moment, I wasn't worried about how all this would end up. I was focused on feeding, drinking, feeding some more.

The check eventually came around, and I went from satiated to nervous as Veronique lightly placed her hand on the check. She looked up at the waiter, something flashing behind her dark eyes.

"I believe there is a discrepancy," she told him.

He bent over to peer at the check, and as he did, Veronique touched his wrist. Her hand glowed red and the waiter fell.

He cracked his head on the table and took one of the plates with him as he slid to the side.

Just as this happened, all the screws and bolts in the restaurant tore from their sockets, followed by anything metal, from silverware to napkin holders.

People started to scream and scramble, the metal whipping around the room like angry bees, scraping the walls and shattering anything it came into contact with.

Oblivious to the chaos, Veronique took my hand and quietly led me out of the restaurant. We passed through the lobby, made it to the elevator, and took the ride up to our penthouse.

Her knees buckled once we reached the door of our room, and she fell into my arms.

"What's wrong?" I asked, my thoughts blurred from the alcohol and pandemonium I'd just witnessed.

Her face was flushed, and I could suddenly smell the sweet sick scent of alcohol.

"Just relax," I told her as I reached for my room key. "Let's get you into bed."

Chapter Fifteen: A Hand in the Shower

Kudos to the waiter for showing up drunk and transferring his drunkenness to Veronique. With both women out – Veronique on the king-sized bed in one room and Grace on the queen-sized bed in the other – I was finally able to focus a little more on my writing.

Of course, it took me all of twenty minutes to calm down and parse through what had happened in the restaurant.

That was some pretty crazy shit, and I couldn't get the image out of my head of Veronique and me moving through the pandemonium as screws and bolts and nails and knives zipped all around us in the air.

There was something beautiful about it; something utterly frightening too. This was another side of the superhero story most people didn't get to experience: what it felt like from a civilian perspective.

So, I was ready for some peace and quiet, and I'd just sat down to write when Veronique stirred.

"What's wrong with me?" She asked as she sat up. Her stomach grumbled as she looked at me, her face bright red.

It wasn't so easy to answer her, especially because there was a flattened coat hanger floating in the air before me.

"You poisoned me," she said, and with the flick of her wrist, the coat hanger shiv began to rotate.

It was aimed at my face, and I knew exactly where it would go if I didn't tell her what she wanted to hear.

The only problem was, I didn't really know what she wanted to hear, nor did I know how to explain everything to her in a way she'd readily understand.

Deep breath in, and I started with the basics. "Do you know what drunk is?"

She didn't nod, but the coat hanger flinched as if to replicate a nod.

"Okay, so you know what drunk is. Good. I mean, bad. Drunk is bad. I think the waiter was drunk," I said, recalling that his eyes had been glazed over and that he'd stumbled a bit on the way to the kitchen.

"You tried to poison me," she slurred.

"Veronique, please, *please* don't fucking stab me with that goddamn hanger."

I thought about swiping the hanger out of the air but quickly bottled that thought, knowing all too well that this would end poorly for me.

Instead, I tried reason.

"Where the hell was I supposed to get some poison over the last couple of hours?" I asked her as calmly as possible. "I have no idea how to poison you, nor anyone for that matter. I mean, aside from making you drink bleach or something, which I clearly don't have the power to do, I'm pretty much clueless when it comes to killing people. Hiding the bodies too. Well, I didn't do too poorly back at the Home Depot parking lot."

"Enough talking," she growled.

"Okay," I said, clearing my throat. "But I just want to be clear: I don't even know what's poisonous, aside from certain snakes, some cleaners, spiders, and, um, mercury. I think mercury is poisonous."

Another deep breath in and I found I wasn't nearly as on edge as I should have been. Oddly enough, I had grown used to being around the superpowered women. I mean, I'm not saying I was all of a sudden some sort of expert, but a lot of weird shit had happened to me over the last few days and as it would turn out, this was just the start of the madness to come.

The clothes hanger lowered to the ground, and she stood. "Maybe you're right. Maybe."

"You should rest," I said, moving to her.

"Sit," she told me as she approached. "What are you going to do now?"

"Well, I was hoping to write a few thousand more words, but like I told you before dinner, my brain is a little fried for that. So I'm going to work on a cover for the book."

"Okay." She sat on her knees and leaned her elbow against my thigh. "Two days."

"Um," I swallowed hard as I realized she'd only have to drop her hand to drain me of my life force. And why was she sitting on the floor next to me?

What in the actual fuck is going on here?

"I want to watch you make a book cover."

"Sure! Great, yes, no problem. You can watch me screw around with these covers."

She yawned, and for the next few minutes, I tried to ignore the fact that she had her elbow on my thigh. I didn't feel any of the energy leaving my body, so at least she hadn't triggered that ability.

I also no longer felt the buzz from the margarita I'd had earlier.

As I'd continue to discover the better I got to know her, Veronique had a third super ability: She could put me on edge, take me off the edge, put me on edge again, and again guide me off in a matter of minutes.

Focus, Writer Gideon, I told myself, pretending it was Grace's voice. Damn, did I miss having her around.

If I had to get this book out in less than two days, the cover wasn't going to be great.

But I could try my best, and thinking of the cover got me thinking about book titles. My first thought for a book title was *Cherry Blossom Girls*, but that sounded stupid, and the cover would have to be really good to convey what it was about.

I then thought about calling the book *Subject S and V,* or maybe, *Subject G and Subject S,* but that also wouldn't fit, and it sounded worse than my first idea.

"What do you think about the title *Mutants in the Making?*" I asked Veronique.

She removed her elbow and lay down on the floor, curling up at my feet. It was an awkward pose for her, and she quickly sat back up, placed her arms on my lap, eventually settling her head on her arms.

What the hell is she doing? I thought as I felt something stir in my groin.

Do not ... do not ... I started to tell my proof of manhood.

Focus, you horny bastard!

"I have to get this cover right," I whispered to myself, as if vocalizing it would distract me from the fact that Veronique was now sleeping with her head in my lap.

Mutants in the Making? It wasn't the best title, but it *was* kind of cool, and if I had a cool subtitle, it would be at least halfway legit.

That one would definitely not work, but 'based on a true story' was a keeper.

My first take at the cover took me too long, which meant that it wasn't spontaneous, wasn't authentic. Besides, it also looked like a damn college macroeconomics textbook. And what the hell were all the *Dr. Mario*-esque pink things?

I toiled around a little more in Photoshop, trying a different idea, a different, sexier approach.

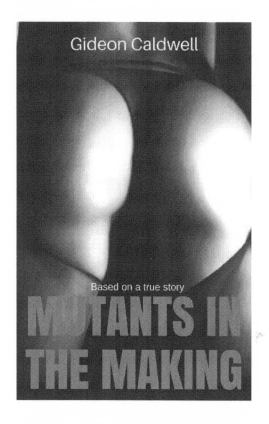

Yep, a throwaway cover for sure. My mind was a blur when I crafted that version, but if this had been an erotic title, that'd be an award-winning cover right there.

Gideon, you are delusional.

I moved on to the next design idea. I wanted this one to be a bit more mainstream, so no thongs, and I wanted it to be a little more poppy.

This one didn't work either. It looked way too amateurish, and I'd spelled my last name wrong too. Also, there wasn't really room for the tagline, so it was a definite no.

So far, I'd had three duds, and one of those duds was just straight up out of left field. I don't even know what I was thinking when I designed the sexy one.

Maybe the alcohol?

I wasn't feeling drunk ten minutes ago, but since Veronique dozed off, a feeling of drunkenness had washed over me.

I was a lightweight, so one margarita would knock me on my ass for sure.

"Two days," I reminded myself. "Actually, less than that now – a lot less. What do you want this book to say? How do you want the cover to come across?"

The things writers ask themselves, am I right?

I tinkered around for another ten minutes, unhappy with the final result:

The font color was atrocious, and I'd messed with the tint so much that I'd lost the feel of the original. Besides, what the hell was it supposed to mean anyway? What did the flower represent? Why did it look wilted?

I decided to get serious with this last one.

I needed a big concept, so I chose a galaxy. It was a good image, and people recognized it as something other, something bigger than themselves.

Next, I needed me, or at least someone that was male, who was supposed to represent me.

In actuality, I was your average bearded writer dude with glasses. That wouldn't work. So, I found a Creative Commons image of a guy who looked better than me. Or at least his silhouette looked better than mine because it didn't have a beard.

I slapped it on that cover, found a badass font, put in all the deets that I needed, and felt the urge to pat myself on the back. I finally had a winner.

With a few more saturation adjustments and some good font spacing, I had myself a cover that Random Penguin House would have been proud to pay fifteen thousand dollars to have designed.

It didn't quite convey the whole 'government super soldier experiment thing' that I wanted to reveal, but I could put that in the product description, and besides, I had to get the book in people's hands *before* I could blow their minds and uncover more of the truth.

Because that's what all this was about, uncovering more of the truth.

"What now, what now?" I asked myself.

I hadn't done badly for the day.

I'd written a crapton of words, found out a lot more about Grace and Veronique, and I'd designed a pretty damn good cover. With enough rest, I could very well finish the book tomorrow.

It would take a ton of coffee, but Veronique didn't say anything about word count, so who cared if the book topped out at thirty thousand words or less? Who said it couldn't be a novella? Who said it couldn't be twenty thousand words?

Then the idea came to me: I would publish the book as a *serial*, each installment detailing how things had changed since the last go around!

It was an accomplishable goal, and it would hopefully have the effect of building an audience.

Of course, there were now thirty million or so self-published works out there, but the fact I'd have a wider net with more books would surely help.

"Veronique," I said softly, "I'm going to move you to the bed. I want to take a shower."

She groaned, looked up at me, and nodded.

"Come on," I said, helping her up. "You can sleep in your clothes, that's no big deal."

I got her to bed, tucking her in like a baby, and stepped into the immaculate bathroom. Sure, I could have run out of the room, Grace over my shoulder, but where would I run? Besides, I felt like Veronique was starting to warm up to me.

I wasn't good with architectural terms, but there was a pretty big counter in the bathroom made of marble and a tub large enough for two, as well as a walk-in shower that was looking real nice right about now.

The water came on with the press of a button on the wall and I stripped down.

I got in and let the warm water hit my body, washing away the day.

I thought back to the erotica-esque cover I had designed, and my hand naturally gravitated toward my member.

Don't do it, I mentally ordered as I started 'cleaning.'

But that never stopped me, and it hardly stopped any man aside from a monk, and even those guys got a little weird after a spell.

Do not masturbate, do not masturbate, I told myself as I began tugging.

I managed to stop, took a deep breath, and tried to just enjoy the hot water and quiet. The day hadn't been as tense as the previous one – if you didn't count Veronique's surprise attack – but I did have this deadline looming over my head, even though I'd figured out a way around it.

I popped open the hotel shampoo, spread it through my hair, and made the split-second decision to give myself another pull.

Do not do it, just take a shower and go to bed.

That was when the shower curtain slipped aside.

Veronique stood before me, completely nude, her arms at her sides and a soft, yet awkward smile on her face.

I nearly slipped backward, hit my head on the wall, and died in a shower at the Marriott in Stamford, Connecticut.

"Do you mind if I join you?"

She was incredibly fit, almost sinewy, and as I took her in, I noted she was clean-shaven and that there was a small birthmark on her hip.

"You should have knocked," I mumbled.

"What were you doing in here?" Her eyes darted to my swollen mini-writer.

"Just cleaning!" I said as I covered myself.

I was so shocked that I hadn't even thought of covering my Johnson when she first opened the curtain.

"It'll go faster if we clean each other," she said, stepping into the shower.

She was petite, slightly bottom-heavy, her breasts much smaller than Grace's, and her nipples large and erect.

But I was trying not to stare, trying my damndest not to stare.

This was one situation I hadn't predicted, not that I predicted much of this, but I'd figured Grace and I would hook up because I felt some chemistry between us. Turns out I was right.

But Veronique and me?

"I'll help you." She ran the soap over my chest.

"I was just finishing up," I grunted.

"Clearly," Veronique said as her hand fell to my proof of manhood.

I closed my eyes; I had no idea how to react to this other than to let it happen, and just … Well, to think that I'd ended up in this situation

… Damn it, Gideon, just enjoy it … Okay, okay that feels good … Yes, yes, focus on the writing, don't focus on …

I felt the strange sensation in my stomach and my eyes popped open. I looked down. Her hand had started to turn red.

"What are you doing?"

"I never tried to take power this way before," she said. "I'll stop."

Veronique removed her hand from my penis. She glanced at the shower head and it moved ever so slightly, spraying the hot water against her chest rather than her neck and chin.

"You don't have to," I said hella awkwardly. "I mean, you don't have to *stop*. You do have to stop using your ability though, because that could kill me."

"I don't think you can handle it," she said coyly.

"Not only do I think you're right, I think you're wrong. I'm much tougher than I, um, look."

Nope, not even I was convinced by that last statement.

"How tough can you be? You're a bearded writer who writes some type of fiction that is fake."

"All fiction is fake. Besides that, did you see the new cover I designed? It's a winner," I said, barely able to swallow my own bullshit.

"I don't think I saw it."

I could tell by her movements that she was still drunk, which was maybe why she decided to join me in the shower. Even though I was entirely turned on by her, I was also very apprehensive, akin to the way a male black widow feels right as he's about to score.

She grabbed me again and began moving her hand up and down.

"What does it feel like?"

"It feels, like, good? Great! I don't really know how to explain how that feels to a female."

"Dicks are interesting. They grow, and they shrink." She flicked the top of my penis. "Yours looks like a long mushroom."

I cleared my throat. "I was not expecting this, Veronique, to be honest with you ..."

"What were you expecting?"

"To take a shower," I said with a sigh. She was stroking fast now and staring at me intently as she did so.

How do you know so much about this? I wanted to ask, but all I could do was exhale deeply.

She kept going and moved just a few inches closer to me. I could now feel a sexual tension radiating off her skin.

It was too much, and I seriously doubt anyone besides a professionally-trained porn star could have lasted as long as I did. Okay, that's a lie, but I gave it my college try and actually lasted another minute as she found a good, steady rhythm.

"I'm going to …"

She stopped and removed her hand. "You have one day to finish the book." She pushed the shower curtain away and started to get out.

"I'm almost finished," I told her quickly. "I have a better idea for releasing the book, and I'm ready to get the first one out by the end of the day tomorrow. Seriously!"

"A better idea?" She stepped back into the shower.

If I could have bit my fist without looking like a total idiot, I would have. I was on the verge of just about everything. The verge of orgasm; the verge of crying out in fear if she didn't like my idea and I wasn't able to finish the book; the verge of embarrassment as I realized the tone of that last thing I'd said sounded like I was begging.

"Yes, a better idea! Sorry, not trying to yell, I just have this release strategy that will allow me – I mean us, to put more books out and hopefully find out about other people who are experiencing this."

"What makes you think people who know about people like me would read your books?" She returned her hand to my confused penis. Damn, it was getting steamy in that shower. It was as if a mist were growing between us.

"I have no idea about that part, but I do think putting it out there will get us some contact from … from maybe someone who has heard about something like this, something similar. You know what, I think it'll give us a lead, and that's what we need. We need to lead – er, *a* lead … we need a lead, dammit."

She began moving her hand up and down again. "And what about the Rose-Lyle facility?"

"You decide what you want to do to it and how you want to do it," I said quickly. "I'll help in any way I can."

"Well, you can drive. Neither of us can drive."

"Then I will be the driver!"

"And you have other skills that you bring to the table. At least, I think you do." She narrowed her eyes at me and stopped jerking her hand.

I gulped. "Um, yeah, I believe I bring other things to the table too."

My god, was I a weakling.

It was amazing to me how much could be done by just grabbing a man's penis and giving him a command.

Veronique could have told me to punch myself in the face at that moment, and I would have done so. She could have told me to deepthroat the hotel shampoo bottle, and I would have swallowed that thing right up.

185

"Do you want me to finish?" she asked, not seeming to feel the water as it bounced off her back.

I nodded, ashamed, but happy to finally get some closure to all this.

Chapter Sixteen: We Will Destroy Them All

I slept like a baby. That was, until a screaming voice woke me up. I'd been dreaming about my superpower, which kept changing as Grace, Veronique, and I fought off some of the MercSecure goons.

In one moment, I had sharp claws, the next I was flying through the air, my body set aflame. At some point in the fight sequence, I learned the ability to kinetically charge things, which I put to my advantage by charging a bus in the midst of our countless enemies.

But the scream inside my head ruined all of that. I practically jump-kicked out of bed, afraid of what I may find, afraid that the government had finally caught up to us.

Veronique was asleep next to me, my sudden movement doing nothing to stir her.

My vision blurred. I glanced around the room again trying to decipher where the sound came from. The morning sun peeked through the blinds, casting a thin crack of light on the door. I was warm; the room was much hotter than I would have liked.

Don't say anything, don't do anything. It's me.

Grace? I thought.

Her voice returned to my head.

Yes, and I have just a little bit of energy now, so I need to use it wisely.

What's with the screaming inside my head?

I thought it would wake you.

I considered this for a moment. *Well, it definitely did. But I thought you had to see me to use your abilities?*

I have imprinted on you, and as of one night ago, you imprinted on me.

That's one way to put it. Look, I know this may sound strange, especially considering the fact that she tried to kill you – well, kill you-ish. But we need to work with Veronique. She seems to want some of the same things we want. Actually, we never really discussed what we wanted, but I'm pretty sure it's the same thing that she wants.

I don't know if that's a good idea. She came after us to take us back to them.

Yeah, but she also killed the people she came with, I thought back.

I see that she has gotten in your mind somewhat, among other places. I would love a shower at the moment.

I gulped as I carefully removed the cover from my body. *I plead the fifth? No, that won't work against you. Look, we spent a lot of time together over the last day, and I'm starting to trust her more than before.*

Is that all it takes for someone to gain your trust? A handjob?

I trusted her before that – you can scour my mind to see for yourself! Okay, so I didn't trust her fully before that, but I trust her a little more now, and she's giving me a day to get this book up and out. And I'm ready. Got the cover ready, and I have a release strategy; we're going to get this story out.

I took a deep breath and turned to Veronique, making sure she was still asleep.

Can't you just imprint on her mind or something? I thought to Grace. *Imprint on her that we are kind of all in this together now and that I'm going to help you two destroy the Rose-Lyle facility and help discover where other superpowered individuals may be. Notice I didn't call you mutants, although that is in the title of the book I'm writing.*

We may be able to work together, but I need to be stronger before I attempt to come out of the coma-like state she's put me in.

How much longer will that take?

Distract her for two more hours? I'm afraid she's going to feed on me when she wakes up, just to get a little more of my energy.

Does she actually need to eat food?

189

Yes and no. Like any human, she does gain sustenance from eating food, but she gains a lot more by draining a person's life force. She prefers that, I believe.

She really is like a vampire, even the way she acts and ...

Seduces. I'm aware. Distract her for two hours, and do not let her feed. Then, I will have leverage, and maybe we can come to some agreement about how we should go forward.

Got it.

"Hey, Veronique." I touched her lightly on the shoulder. Her eyes popped open and she glared at me for a moment before her scowl softened at the edges.

"Are you ready to start writing?" she said, instead of good morning.

"Yeah, I am, but first I want to do something amazing."

"Amazing?"

I gave her the most sincere shit-eating grin I could muster. "This hotel has the grandest, most beautiful breakfast buffet you could possibly imagine. We call it a continental breakfast, and it truly is continental."

"Is it now?"

"Oh, yeah, it is a great breakfast, Grace and I had it yesterday. You just have to try it. You'll be so impressed. I know it's not maybe what you would normally eat, but I think you'll love it, and I would love to be able to make you something."

She sat up, her interest piqued. "Make me something?" She wore a training bra and nothing else beneath the blanket. Her demeanor was totally the opposite of what it had been in the shower; I no longer had the sense that I could reach out and touch her if I wanted.

Which was possibly a good thing.

I nodded, the grin still on my face. "That's right, I want to make you an amazingly delicious extra sweet waffle. And while you're eating that, I'll make you a plate of bacon and sausage and potatoes and eggs and … Hell, I'll probably be able to get you some yogurt, and some orange juice, and some coffee, and maybe even some fruit."

She licked her lips. "That doesn't sound too bad …"

I smiled at her. "It's going to be phenomenal; the best breakfast you've ever had. It's a continental breakfast – I mean, when was the last time you had a continental breakfast?"

"Never."

"Exactly! Let's go down there and have ourselves a badass breakfast, and then I'll get back up here and start writing. No, you know what? Let's have some breakfast, then go for a quick walk to get motivated – because that's important – and then we'll come back and I'll get started."

"I think that will be fine, yes."

191

Thank you, Gideon, Grace's voice said in my skull as I got out of bed. *Are you sure you're not a psychic?*

No, I've just learned how to bullshit well, I responded as I put my pants on.

After Veronique slipped back into her tight, black mil-spec outfit, we headed down to the breakfast buffet. I wore a turtleneck sweater and a pair of jeans with holes at the knees. We were definitely mismatched, an odd couple, but no one at the buffet seemed to care.

To prolong our time at the buffet, I told Veronique it was customary for people to take items one at a time.

Of course, the hungry Americans all around me proved me wrong, but she didn't seem to notice this. She had lightened up since the day before, and while she wasn't smiling at me per se, there was a mischievous, yet friendly, look to her eyes.

We didn't discuss what happened in the bathroom last night, and I was glad for that.

Mostly, we ate and drank, and I continued to try to make time pass, checking the clock on my phone every now and then. I suggested a walk, a look in the hotel's gift shop, a tour of the guest amenities. She agreed to everything.

About two hours later, we took the elevator back to our suite.

Get ready, Grace's voice said inside my head.

I tensed up, took a deep breath, and opened the door to our room.

Everything about the room was the same as it was before. Veronique, however, noticed that I was apprehensive.

"Are you okay?"

"Yes! I was just thinking about what I was going to write. I get tense like this sometimes before I write."

"Okay," she said, brushing past me.

I swallowed hard and moved over to my laptop, trying to stay as nonchalant as possible.

"Just going to do some writing," I said.

Veronique stopped in front of the bed. Her eyes flashed and she hit the mattress, lying there as if she'd gone into a trance.

My heart skipped a beat as Grace stepped into the room. She looked calm and poised, her eyes white, her pupils tiny black dots.

"I don't want you to hurt her," I told Grace. "I know more about you two now, and I need both of you – *we* need both of you."

"She can kill us." Grace moved toward me, her shoulders swaying as she walked.

She was incredibly beautiful … her long blonde hair, her blue eyes, her voluptuous figure.

She wore an outfit similar to Veronique's, a tight mil-spec number with a zipper on the front. Of course, she'd only zipped it up to about the meeting point of her breasts, almost as if it were a dominatrix bodysuit.

It was a fantasy outfit, that was for sure, likely something she pulled from my mind and juxtaposed with Veronique's getup.

It almost reminded me of something one of the X-Men would wear, which, as I moved further into my adult life, became more and more ridiculous. I mean, all superheroes, no matter which publisher, wore pretty ridiculous outfits. But then again, if they didn't wear those crazy outfits, would we like them as much?

"Quiet, Writer Gideon," Grace said as she glowered at Veronique. "Your internal banter is distracting me."

"No, I'm serious here," I said, standing my ground. "We've got enough problems, and I don't want to add you two fighting each other to our list. For example, we need to check out by eleven a.m., or go downstairs and trick them again using your abilities. My point is: both of you are a key to this puzzle, and both of you have powers that we need to use together, to stop them."

"He's right," Veronique gasped. Her eyes flashed back to their normal color and then turned white again.

"Grace, let her go. And Veronique, don't do anything crazy when she does. Someone needs to take charge here, and, um, that person is going to have to be me."

Surprisingly, the tone of my voice seemed to completely change Grace's demeanor. There was still anger in her eyes but also a strange sense of obedience. Which there shouldn't have been, because she could have fileted my mind if she had wanted.

Grace's shoulders relaxed, and Veronique slipped off the bed and stood in one fluid motion, her stance that of a person ready to kill.

"Okay everyone," I said, holding my hands out wide, palms facing the two women. "Let's just bring this down a notch. I need to finish my book, first off. And you two need to give me as much information as you can without fighting or killing each other."

"Nice to see you, *Grace*," Veronique said. While her normally harsh tone wasn't evident, there was still something there, something slightly aggressive in her voice.

Grace glared at her. "It wasn't nice what you did to me."

"You would have done the same to me."

"But now we're one big happy family, and I need you two to behave," I said. "Now, Veronique, you need to get some new clothes. Grace, you have the ability to help her get new clothes."

"I could find one of the hotel maids," Grace said.

"Yes, you could. In fact ..." Something occurred to me. "I know you were trying to make a suggestion that you would get Veronique some maid clothing, which is not what we need. But it does give me an idea. We can't go around wearing private security uniforms. We've

195

done that twice now," I said to Veronique. "It'll raise suspicion. I'll call room service and send a maid up. Grace, have them buy clothing for Veronique."

"Okay."

"I need to get like eight thousand more words written," I told them. "And to do that, I'm going to need some concentration time, so what I want to happen here is for you, Veronique, to stay in this room and just relax while the maid is out buying you new clothes. Grace, I need you to come in the other room with me so I can ask you some questions."

"Fine."

I shook my head at her. "And I know you've been either modifying the truth or lying to me some. So that ends now. The truth from now on. I checked your drive while you were out. Give me the truth, got it?"

Veronique grinned at her counterpart. "I let him access you."

"And one more thing, Veronique, no more deadline. This book will be finished today, but that's because I want to publish it as a serial. So can it with the threats. We'll get the book out today, we'll make some plans for tomorrow, and we'll go from there."

I was surprised that it was Grace who spoke up next, especially after what she said. "We will destroy the facility."

It'd been less than a day without the psychic and I'd already forgotten just how powerful she was.

"Exactly, we'll destroy the facility and we'll uncover the truth, even if it kills us. Hopefully, we'll find more of them," I said, my voice increasing in volume. "And we'll go for them too. We'll destroy them all."

"Yes," Veronique said, "we will."

"Your skills will come in handy for gathering info, Grace, but we also need to rely on the collective readership of America, because there are a lot of people in places that we have no access to. People may know more about these experiments and the people who are being experimented on. So let's get started."

Veronique moved back to the bed and sat, then turned on the TV.

"Good, that's the spirit," I said, my voice faltering.

After you're done asking me questions, can I watch daytime television too? Grace's voice echoed in my head.

I couldn't help but laugh. "Definitely. But I want to experiment some more with adjusting your stats first. I think it may come in handy in the future. And I want to know why my picture was on your hard drive. How is that even possible?"

Grace shrugged. "We'll just have to find out."

Chapter Seventeen: Memories Revisited

Grace and I went downstairs to extend our stay another day, which was a piece of cake. The next thing to do was get some clothing. We found a maid stepping out of one of the rooms on the floor below us.

"Tell her to get some nice clothes, a lot of nice clothes."

"She doesn't have any money on her," Grace explained as she read her mind. "She doesn't have a lot in her bank either."

"Crap, I didn't consider that. You know what? Let's just deal with clothing later. Veronique's military black will work for now. Disregard what I said earlier about it making her stand out. I mean, it's America, people wear crazy things all the time."

"Is my outfit crazy?" she asked. The maid stood before us, still in a trance. Grace was now in a coat, my pants, and a sweater with a cherry blossom stitched on it.

This got me wondering just how Grace chose clothing. For people, she had to have seen them once before. Was it the same for clothing? Or could she think anything up and it worked?

I tried to get this answer out of her as we went back to our room, but she didn't give me much detail about it.

"Sorry, no clothes for now, Veronique," I told the deadly woman relaxing in front of the TV. She was glued to the screen, watching a rerun of some *Big Bang Theory* spinoff.

Once we got into the second bedroom, Grace lay on the bed and I used my phone to plug into the port on her neck. Her head was propped up by a single pillow, her blue eyes gazing steadily at me.

"You don't have to watch me," I told her, feeling just a hint of nervousness.

"I've had my eye on you for a few days now," she said with a chuckle.

"I believe that."

The first thing I did was bring up her psychic stats. They were presented to me the way they had been the second time, with dials that I could adjust.

Omnikinesis: 1

Second Sight: 1

Psychometry: 5

Telepathy: 8

Clairsentience: 7

Psychokinesis: 1

Hypnosis: 6

It was time for me to research a little more about what these things were. With my laptop open, I researched each skill individually, figuring it would fill out my manuscript.

A few of them, such as Second Sight, were self-explanatory. I knew what telepathy was and I was familiar with psychokinesis and hypnosis.

Psychometry was interesting; it allowed her to touch an object or a person and understand that person's emotional state or the history behind the object. Like, she could touch Hunter S. Thompson's typewriter, and learn more about his years of drug abuse.

Clairsentience was the ability to figure out past, present, and future emotional states of people. This would come in handy in the future – a future in which I hoped to use her powers to their utmost ability.

It became clear as I read more about omnikinesis that I had finally stumbled upon a min-max situation. Omnikinesis was all of the psychic abilities combined and increasing it increased the other powers as well.

This became evident as I turned all the other ones down and adjusted Omnikinesis up to ten.

The results brought a smile to my face.

As soon as omnikinesis hit ten, all the other skills jumped to either five or six, so that her dials looked like this:

Omnikinesis: 10

Second Sight: 5

Psychometry: 5

Telepathy: 6

Clairsentience: 5

Psychokinesis: 7

Hypnosis: 5

Psychokinesis, which had been at one before, had surprisingly jumped up to seven. So this wasn't a min-max situation at all; it was a situation in which someone had turned down her best ability to prevent the other abilities from being higher.

There was a ton of other stuff I wanted to do while plugged into her, but I couldn't resist testing her psychokinesis ability.

"Grace, I want you to use your mind to lift that TV."

"Use my mind to lift the TV?" She looked from me to the flat screen television on the nightstand.

"Yes. I've been messing with your psychic abilities a bit, and I think this is something you may be able to do now. Focus on it, and, um, pick it up with your mind."

Talk about becoming a Jedi master – I had just made the leap from Padawan to Yoda in a matter of seconds.

Grace's brow furrowed, and her eyes flashed white as she looked at the television. The television wobbled, lifted, fell back to the nightstand, and lifted again, this time floating a good two feet into the air.

"That's awesome!"

She gently set the television down. "Really?"

"Really." A few thoughts raced through my mind and I settled on the most logical. "Okay, I want you to try a heavier object. Fuck, try me. That's it – lift me! Lift me up with your abilities, but not too high because I'm afraid of heights. Kidding, but seriously, try."

I stood with my hands at my side, ready to see how powerful she truly was.

I felt a tingling sensation in my stomach as my feet lifted off the ground. "Keep going," I told her, a smile on my face. She continued lifting me until I was a few feet from the ceiling. I reached my hand up and touched it for stability.

"This is so sweet," I breathed. "But as much as I'd like to float around the room like Peter Pan, I have more work to do. You can lower me now, we need to continue."

Using the smartphone, I began going through some of the subfolders in search of data that could possibly help us. I also wanted to ask her questions that would help expand my manuscript and expose more of what was going on at the secret Rose-Lyle facility.

"You're wasting your time," she told me.

"By going through your data? What about the fact that I found my pictures in there? I just have so many questions about this."

"Maybe it would be better if I showed you."

"You mean transfer …" I made a gesture that meant mind to mind. "Sure, it would kick ass if you could show me something that helped me better understand what you experienced. But we need a safe word because if you show me too much and I feel like I'm trapped, it could be a traumatizing experience."

"It was a traumatizing experience."

I considered that for a moment. "Yeah, you're right; you should just show me," I said bravely.

"Come lay down next to me."

Grace didn't have to ask me twice. I unplugged my phone, wrapped the cable around it, and got on the bed next to her.

I swallowed hard as she placed her hand on mine. "Close your eyes."

My lids shut tight and a myriad of moving images came to me.

It was not at all like watching a video, or a flashback.

It was like waking up in the middle of the night and thinking of everything at once – your past, your future, something that occurred recently, something that occurred months ago, and something that could potentially happen. A literal wall of memory slammed into me.

I understood Grace's life now, at least the life that she wanted to share with me.

Because of her psychic ability, she was kept in solitary confinement from the age of three or four to her current age of twenty-one.

She'd been given things to watch and books to read, but she wasn't allowed to actually interact with others, aside from two scientists, and only then if she was blindfolded.

They used robots and later androids, primitive ones, to communicate with her. Her best friend growing up was an Android from Japan that could do little more than answer simple questions and do funny dances. Because of this robot, I found out, she spoke Japanese.

While in solitary confinement, Grace had been observed by dozens of security cameras set up in clusters in the corners. There was also a room with one-way mirrors that she would be taken to every week.

This was what made her so different from Veronique, who seemed to have more interaction with people and was allowed to go out once she became older.

"It's so terrible," I said as I felt what it must have been like to be sheltered from the world for so long. She wasn't starved or anything, and no one had ever done anything to harm her; she was simply kept in utter isolation.

It was a wonder this government lab didn't raise a feral human being.

If it hadn't been for her constant media consumption, she would have been fucked in the head. I mean she was already slightly fucked in the head, but she was sweet, and she generally seemed to mean well.

The media consumption also helped her with her shifter abilities. The scientists had made sure her voice remained the same no matter what form she took. This was so she couldn't confuse them, and it was also why the setting was so low when I first examined her.

Everything was starting to make sense.

"How did you escape?" I whispered. "How did you end up at my doorstep?"

Those images came to me as well, swirling around my mind as if they were a flock of birds being stalked by an eagle.

Grace had planned her escape for over a year.

She didn't have much contact with anyone, aside from a pair of scientists. These scientists would speak to her every couple of days, together, and they made sure she was blindfolded, wore a helmet with the visor blacked out, and that her hands were shackled. A robot did the shackling.

I intuited most of these things through the transfer of her memory. Because her eyes were shut, she couldn't see what the two scientists looked like, but as our minds are prone to do when only give a portion of the details, hers quickly filled in the rest.

One of the scientists had a weaker will than the other, this she was sure of.

The cuffs they made her wear weren't tight, and she could move around; they were mainly given to prevent her from touching someone and understanding their memories, which would have allowed her to manipulate them.

So this became her next mission: get them to remove the cuffs.

After several months of very soft complaining, she finally got the two scientists to meet her without the cuffs.

She was clever enough not to ever move in a way that seemed aggressive or confrontational, and she kept this act up for three months, uncuffed in a room with the two scientists.

The scientists continued to grow more casual around her, especially the one she'd sensed was weak, and it was on a dark and stormy night that she finally made her move.

As the first scientist took his seat, Grace dove toward him, still completely blindfolded. She missed his body entirely but was able to grab onto his ankle, and from there slid her hand up his pant leg and touched his skin.

The rest was history.

The scientist turned to his counterpart and beat the living hell out of him. After that, the possessed man helped Grace up and removed her visor and blindfold.

This was an especially powerful moment for her, when the dark turned to light and she could put a face to the man's voice. What a strange feeling that must have been.

Why were you naked when you came to my door? I thought.

The answer came almost before I could get the question out.

Grace was usually naked at the facility because of the fact that she could form her own clothing. And, as she became aware that the planned escape was going in her favor, she quickly morphed into the scientist's counterpart.

She told him to take her to his car.

She had no idea where to have him take her, and they were circling through Wooster Square to get to the highway when she momentarily lost her grip on his psyche.

In that instant, he verbally told his car to call work and tell them Grace had escaped. It only took her a second after that to regain control over him again. But rather than have him drive her any longer – knowing they'd be looking for her – she made him pull over.

Grace then wiped his thoughts and told him to drive to as far away as possible.

Being free, and in a place she didn't recognize, was utterly terrifying. She lost it then and started screaming for help, which caused her to again lose focus and return to her base, naked form. This explained why she was nude when I met her, and it also explained why she wouldn't let me phone the police.

"So, that's your story," I said as she finished showing me.

"Yes."

"I don't know why you came to me, but I'll do my best to make it right." I sat up and looked at her. She moved a bit closer to kiss me. The hair on my neck stood at attention as I thought about Veronique in the other room.

"Later, I need to work now."

Chapter Eighteen: Heavy Metal Orchestra

Me: Luke, the story is just getting crazier and crazier.

Luke: Where you at wordcount-wise?

Me: I've been going at it since about eleven, and I'm passing the twenty-three thousand mark. I got a whole new release strategy involved, a serial of sorts.

Luke: Serials seem to be pretty hit or miss.

Me: True, but with the story I have, and its implications, I need to put it out there in concentrated doses. Having more of a reach through multiple releases may help with that, but it's too early to be sure.

Luke: So, what's happening in the story then? Did you get some action in?

Me: Action is coming, right now I'm working on the build-up to an action scene. My three protagonists are going to destroy the secret government facility that created the two superpowered women.

Luke: Do you have an antagonist yet?

Me: Not really, aside from an ambiguous government operation and a security company called MercSecure.

Luke: Well, you'll need someone, maybe an evil professor or something, or a badass, superpowered hombre.

Me: Canadians use the word 'hombre?'

Luke: Lol. They do now! Have you added more game elements yet? I'll take a look at them if you'd like me to.

Me: Readers that like a lot of stats won't be into it, but maybe they'll like the story. There are stats though, and I've figured out a way to adjust them. Let me rephrase: my MC didn't know how to adjust them before, and he still has Veronique, the dangerous one, to work on and modify a bit.

Luke: And is the harem in full effect?

Me: Well, in a way, but the MC isn't … That's not his MO, although it looks like it could move into a polyamorous situation. Hopefully. Who doesn't want to get laid by powerful women?

Luke: Lol. Hopefully? What do you mean hopefully? You're the writer!

Me: These characters have long since taken over, I'm just letting them write their own story now.

As if to prove my point, the front door to our room splintered opened and two smoke grenades tumbled inside.

"Get down!" Veronique screamed at us. The smoke grenades went off, followed by a flashbang.

I heard whooshing sounds as metal seared through the air toward the open door.

I couldn't see it, but I could hear all the metal in the front room being torn from the walls, the television, the light fixtures, and the door. That noise was followed by the sound of screaming men.

Smoke billowed into the second room.

With my laptop now under my arm, I grabbed Grace's hand and asked, "Do you think you can lower us to the ground? We'll get out of this, dammit, just focus!"

Just seeing my determined face brought a sense of calm to her. Her eyebrows lowered.

"Get your things," she said, "Veronique and I will handle this."

Unable to see the security detail, Grace's only option was to use her recently improved psychokinetic abilities. She lifted her hands, and as she did, the walls next to the door collapsed inward. I heard more crunching sounds as the walls in the hallway, and portions of the floor began to crack.

Veronique skidded into our room, her hand over her mouth.

"You can do that now?" she asked.

"Yep, we need to get out of here!" I answered for Grace.

With the smoke starting to billow all around us, there was only one way out. I pointed to the window. Grace nodded, and as she tightened her fist, the window blew out.

And that was when we saw the fucking helicopter approaching the hotel.

"We have to jump!" I told both of them, my nerves on fire, my lungs burning, the smoke from the grenades searing my eyes.

The helicopter, its blades beating loudly, got into position. I hit the deck as bullets ricocheted into the room.

That was it, we were dead. I knew it was over, and I felt ashamed at how poorly it had ended.

But only a few of the bullets managed to reach the far side of the room. The rest stopped mid-air, Veronique's metal wielding power at full capacity.

I watched from my covered position on the floor as the bullets turned back to the helicopter.

"Oh shit!" I whisper-screamed.

A direct headshot into the pilot sent the helicopter crashing against the side of the hotel, its propellers whipping at the window a few doors down and causing a small explosion which rained debris down on the streets below.

"I need more energy!" Veronique was now on one knee, panting.

I put one hand on Grace's shoulder and stared deeply into her ice blue eyes. "Grace, you're our only hope of getting out of here," I told her through clenched teeth. "Please, focus – you can do this!"

Her eyes flashed white, and as she stared at me defiantly, all three of us lifted into the air. I barely managed to grab my duffle bag before we floated over to the blown-out window.

As we reached the window, one of the security personnel shouldered into the room with his weapon drawn. As soon as he saw Grace he turned the weapon on himself, sticking it in his mouth and ending it right there.

"Feed, Veronique!" I called to her, and sensing what I meant, she used her metal ability to drag the soldier closer to her.

Her hand came over what was left of his face. It flashed red, and the man's body began shriveling.

"Are you ready, Grace!?" I shouted.

"Let me get us halfway there," Veronique said. The red power around her fingertips dissipated and color returned to her face.

The floor shook as metal peeled from the building's exterior. The bars of metal twisted in the air outside, forming a primitive staircase.

Grace floated us out the window and set our bodies on the first metal 'stair' that Veronique had created.

The world spun around me as we started moving downward, gravity pulling at us, Yours Truly scared beyond shitless.

Looking back, I think the only thing that kept me from falling over was Grace's ability. There was simply no way a guy like me could run down a makeshift staircase made from building materials as a goddamn Apache helicopter approached us from a distance.

"We've got to get to the BMW!" I yelled wildly, which sounded way cooler in retrospect than it did coming out of my mouth as a pansied shriek.

The Apache moved closer to us, its blades slicing through the air.

Veronique swiped one arm behind her and all the stair pieces we'd already stepped on flew like spears toward the helicopter.

The adrenaline surging through me by this point would have been hard to measure. I started feeling faint, and just before I could fall over the side, Grace lifted me in the air and we lowered the rest of the way to the ground.

We landed and started running. I heard sirens … far away but drawing closer. And another helicopter. It was like something out of a Jerry Bruckheimer film.

We weren't far from the concierge lot when I suddenly remembered that the valet had the keys.

"Grace, keys!" I shouted.

Luckily, the valet was huddled behind his little booth, his hands over his head.

As soon as Grace saw him, he stood up, found our keys, and tossed them to me. No, I didn't have the skill set at that point to catch the keys mid-air, especially with what was going on all around me.

But I had Veronique.

The keys flew into her hand and we dashed down into the winding concierge parking lot.

"Where's our car, where's our car, where's our car?" I mumbled as we ran. I'd never run so fast in my life. It was amazing what a man could do when he had a covert government agency on his ass!

But I'd be winded soon, I could tell, and I was happy as shit when Grace reached out and touched my keys, instantly recalling where the car was parked.

One minute later, we found the beamer. I jumped into the driver's seat, Veronique in the back and Grace at my side.

We tore out of the parking lot, and just as we got to street level, a black SUV with a siren in the window drove onto the scene. It was followed by three more black SUVs and a fucking black Humvee.

The high-speed chase had begun.

"Grace, distract the SUVs!"

I pressed the button on the center panel that brought the top down and looked in the rearview mirror at Veronique, who was already turned around, plotting her next move. "Veronique, take out anyone you can and don't let any of those bullets get to us! Bullets, focus on the bullets!"

She simply nodded without looking back at me.

With my foot on the gas pedal, and my hair whipping in the wind, I swerved around the cars waiting to get onto the highway.

The BMW was fast, and I wasn't the best driver, but I'd played a lot of the first person driving video games. Which really shouldn't count for anything, but I reminded myself of my video game background just for the sake of courage.

Swerving around a red Toyota Corolla, we took the on-ramp to the highway.

As soon as Grace turned and saw the face of a shocked driver, she forced him to lurch right, cutting off one of the SUVs behind us and causing a collision. The other SUVs and the Humvee narrowly avoided this distraction, but they didn't avoid Veronique's next attack.

With her hand raised ever so slightly, she stripped two of the SUVs of their lug nuts. The tires flew off the vehicles, leaving nothing but their frames to scrape against the asphalt as they skidded along the highway.

Sparks flew behind me; it looked like the damn Fourth of July kicking off in my rearview mirror. A barrage of horns, vehicles screeching to a halt, and people shouting. Heavy metal orchestra.

We needed to escape.

But before I got on the phone to Walter White, I had to ditch the BMW. The fact that there were now two helicopters on our asses, and more black SUVs likely to follow, meant it would be easier said than done.

As we sped along I-95 north toward New Haven, reaching speed limits of up to a hundred miles per hour, our next move came to me in a flash.

I knew there was a gas station truck stop about a mile up. We'd take the off-ramp, hit the gas station – well not literally hit it, but get close to hitting it – ditch the beamer, get in an eighteen-wheeler and have Grace take over from there.

It would be very difficult, especially with the helicopters, but those …

I hated to think of it this way, *but those could be dealt with.*

"Veronique!" I called over the roar of the wind and the sounds of the other vehicles. "Try to take out one of those helicopters!"

I watched in the rearview mirror as Veronique looked for things she could fling at the helicopters. They were still pretty far away, and they would need to get closer for us to be able to do anything. What was more, our exit was looming in the distance.

A new idea came to me. "Grace, cause some type of pile up to prevent any more SUVs from following us. We can take out the helicopters at the gas station if we need to."

"Will do."

Grace unbuckled her seatbelt, turned around and got on her knees, her front body pressed against the seat back. She could now see the other drivers around us, and as she looked at each of them, they started slowing down and forming a long, horizontal line.

Any driver she saw came under her spell and got into the line, which would at least give the SUVs trouble.

Now for the helicopters.

We pulled into the gas station and I saw the eighteen-wheeler I wanted to hijack. The driver was just getting in, and the vehicle was aimed at the highway.

"That's our new ride." We got out of the car. I grabbed my duffle bag and gave it to the psychic. "Grace, go get that driver under your control. Veronique, let's do something about those helicopters."

The helicopters were now above the off-ramp, closing in on us. This was a bad move on their part, because the closer they got to us, the easier it was for Veronique to take them out.

With her hands at her side, palms up, Veronique lifted one of the medium-sized metal gas tank lids off the ground with her power.

As if it were a frisbee, she hurled the yellow lid at the first helicopter.

It shattered the window and decapitated the pilot, causing the helicopter to crash in a massive explosion. This was followed by more screams, cars screeching on the highway, and people all around us panicking.

"Hurry!" I told Veronique.

The other helicopter began to push away, only to receive the same treatment, this time with the metal lid taking off the rotor mast. Gravity dragged the second helicopter's tail rotor under and the craft went belly up, smashing into a highway barrier.

By this point, we were in the cab of the eighteen-wheeler, and Grace had the driver under her control. Even as people flipped their shit all around us, we were able to get back on the highway with New Haven as our destination.

It's time to put an end to all this, I thought as my nerves settled, and I was finally able to breathe. I figured the pileup we caused behind us would make the rest of our trip easier.

If only things were that simple.

Chapter Nineteen: Angel

I knew there would be other superpowered individuals, but I didn't think they'd be coming after us so soon. I didn't think they would be able to fly, or have superhuman strength, or the ability to heal.

I happened to be looking in the rear-view mirror when it happened.

Something that resembled a comet crashed down onto the trailer of the eighteen-wheeler, separating it from our cabin, and sending the top portion of the trailer up and over.

The cabin tipped and was dragged to the right, where it quickly flipped onto its side and slid along the highway, as the four of us fell against each other.

Worse yet, it had fallen over onto my side of the cab, and Grace, Veronique, and the driver were all pressed against me.

It settled. I barely had time to suck in a breath when a gloved hand punched through the window and grabbed the hypnotized driver by his neckbeard. The sudden punch also sent a thick piece of glass skittering across the cabin directly into my face.

"Fuck!" The shard connected just an inch or so away from my eye, the eye itself protected by the frame of my glasses.

"Gideon!" Veronique said, trying to squirm around to check on me. All three of us were pressed together, Veronique on top, Grace in the middle, and me on the bottom.

She actually cares? I would have been touched if not for the fact that the situation had taken a turn for the worse.

"I'll be fine." I wiped my face on my arm. "What hit us? A comet? Whose hand was that?"

The vehicle jittered as the gloved hand yanked the driver out of the shattered window, slicing his gut on the jagged glass as he was lugged through the opening.

"It's Angel," Grace gulped, and with that, her eyes flashed white and she blew off the driver's side door.

It was like my writer buddy Luke had read ahead. Whatever was out there was our villain, and action was imminent. Hell, death was imminent too.

Veronique pulled herself toward the open doorway, followed by Grace, followed by me with a bloodied face and my duffle bag over my shoulder.

Looking back, I don't know how I had the wherewithal to bring my bag.

I wasn't dumb enough *not* to write in the cloud, but I still needed my laptop with me to handle all the other publishing aspects.

All of which was stupid to think about, especially as I took in the sight of a muscular man in a mil-spec body suit standing on top of a cratered car next to our overturned cab.

Angel had long dark hair, the majority of which was covering his face.

His features, from his beard stubble to his dark skin, gave him a Mediterranean male look. His black, armored bodysuit was similar to the one that Veronique still wore except his was more muscled and covered with flexible graphene plates.

"What are his powers?" I asked, in awe of the man standing before us.

Pieces of metal began to lift to the air and surround us as Veronique said, "His powers are strength, healing, and he can fly."

With the swipe of her hand, Veronique used her power to hurl the bits of metal at him.

They hit Angel in the chest, sending him up and over the car. But I knew the victory was short-lived when he lifted into the air, his arms at his sides. He dipped his head toward us, a furious look on his face.

Veronique stepped in front of us. "You two go, I will hold him off."

With everything that was happening all around me – from the chaos to the accident we'd just experienced – I hadn't been able to connect an emotion to what was going on.

Now I could.

Veronique's act of bravery snapped me out of my shock and stupor. I suddenly wanted nothing more than to help her, to be there for her.

"We can't leave her behind!" I told Grace. The mysterious woman who'd first shown up at my doorstep looked at me, utter fear on her face as she grabbed my wrist.

"We have to," she said, her voice quivering. "We can't beat him here."

Veronique moved forward, a vortex of metal swirling over her head. "Go!" she shouted to us.

"But we can't!" I cried out, the slice on my cheek pulsing with my heartbeat. I wiped more blood from my face to my arm.

"We'll go after her before they can terminate her or anything else," Grace said quietly. She took a deep breath and continued, "My abilities don't fully work on Angel, but I was able to see that his intentions are not to kill her; he's here to take her back to the facility."

"But –"

Grace tightened her grip on my wrist. "Listen to what I say."

I would recognize later that this was just a formality; Grace didn't have to say anything to take over my mind.

But it was nice of her to at least be polite about it.

223

If I'd had a bird's-eye view of what followed, I would have seen my eyes flash white.

I would have seen Grace leading me away as Veronique went to meet Angel. I would have seen my hypnotized ass dragging one of the drivers affected by the overturned eighteen-wheeler out of their car. I would have seen Grace getting in the passenger seat, me starting up the vehicle, and stepping on the gas pedal.

I would have seen myself driving away, looking at Angel and Veronique clashing in my rearview mirror.

We got all the way to New Haven before Grace let me have my mind back.

Chapter Twenty: Stitched Up

Without Veronique, I didn't know how we would do all this. I was glad Grace had me park before she returned my ability to make rational decisions. She was smart enough not to give me my mind back on the highway, which would have proved disastrous.

As soon as my mind was my own, I punched the steering wheel, not even caring that we'd made it to downtown New Haven. Oblivious to my surroundings, I cursed, shuddering when I thought about what we'd just been through, before finally turning to Grace.

"We shouldn't have left her," I said through gritted teeth.

"We can't take on Angel that way," she said calmly. "I'm not strong enough, not yet, even with the way you adjusted my abilities. I have learned so much being here in the real world with you."

The way she said 'real world' really dug into my core. I was finally starting to understand just how odd this all must be for her, to go from solitary confinement to a high-speed chase in under a week.

At the same time, I still couldn't forgive us for leaving Veronique behind.

"You two should have worked together," I told her. "You could have taken him together."

"I … I don't know. It was so sudden."

"I wish I had one of your powers," I mumbled as I watched a homeless man approach our stolen vehicle.

She grimaced. "No, you don't."

"I could have done something …"

"It doesn't matter."

I thought of Angel again, his hair whipping in the wind, the sullen look on his face. A quote from East of Eden resonated at the back of my skull: "To a monster the norm must seem monstrous, since everyone is normal to himself."

Boy if that didn't fit …

The homeless guy knocked on the window, asking for change. He had on an oversized trench coat and a dirty beanie. Since we needed to ditch the car anyway, and since there was a nice hotel nearby, I figured now was as good a time as any.

"What happened to your face, man?" he asked as I stepped out of the car.

"Grace?" I said as she got out on her side. She had taken the form of the kimonoed Asian woman from my wall.

Her eyes flashed white and the homeless man took the keys from me. "Sure, man, I'll drive this car to Hartford."

"Drive it to Vermont," I said.

"Great, Vermont," was his reply.

He got in and drove off.

"That was easy enough," I said. I took a shirt from my duffle bag and dabbed at the blood on my face.

"We need to do something about your face," Grace said.

She wasn't lying. This cut was deeper than I thought, and portions of my beard were already covered in dried blood.

"Let's just get to the hotel, and hopefully no one really notices us."

"Will they have medical help at the hotel?"

"That's a good question." I glanced around the area and realized we weren't far from the Yale medical school. If there was a nurse or someone who could stitch up a wound, it'd be at Yale. I figured we could walk into the school and Grace could use her ability to find the right person to stitch me up.

She wasn't so sure, and I couldn't blame her, considering I had a face that was bleeding out. But she trusted me, and I quickly led us in that direction, trying to cover my face and keep its view from incoming traffic.

We approached the first building that looked most like a hospital and waltzed right in. The place smelled of antiseptics, and its color palate could have been described as 'bland,' but I'd never been happier in my life to see light turquoise, beige, and pistachio.

Grace went to work.

Like this was the latest primetime medical thriller, a team of nurses came at the call of the front desk woman. I'd never had a chance to adequately count how many people Grace could mind wash at once, but if the medical staff were any indication, it was at least ten.

They put me on a stretcher and rolled me into an operating room. No paperwork was taken – also thanks to Grace – and it wasn't long before a female doctor, a Muslim woman with caramel skin, dark eyes, and a purple hijab, came into the room and started stitching me up.

Talk about cheap health care.

"It's going to leave a scar," was the only thing the woman said to me. "I'm sorry there isn't more I can do."

I shrugged her off. "Well, I shouldn't have fallen down … those stairs. Nope, I shouldn't have fallen down those stairs and landed on something sharp. I'll be more careful next time." Once she finished, she smiled at me and quickly left the room.

"Your abilities are amazing," I told Grace for what must have been the thousandth time as we exited the room and turned back to the main lobby.

She only nodded at this.

I found a bathroom and excused myself, eager to get a look at my face.

Needless to report, Mrs. Caldwell's little boy had finally grown up.

My hair was disheveled, there was a gnarly scar on my face, and my beard was as unkempt as ever. I was ready for my mug shot, ready to become an extreme wrestler, and possibly join a biker gang.

Keep dreaming, Writer Gideon.

"You aren't supposed to be in my mind," I said and thought at the same time.

Hurry.

I knew I needed to change the look up a little more just to keep them guessing, so as we quickly walked back toward downtown New Haven, I stopped in at a barbershop – a black one, I was feeling tough! – and had my head shaved.

I don't know what they thought about the hipster looking dude with the gnarly scar on his face, but I did hear some guy mention I was the toughest looking white boy he'd seen all day.

"It's not too bad," Grace said when we left the barbershop. "Can I touch it?"

I stopped, and she rubbed my head for a moment.

"No shifting in public," I reminded her.

I was hungry, and now that I looked like a badass, there was a lot to be done.

Our top priority was infiltrating the Rose-Lyle facility and rescuing Veronique before they put her out of commission. The next step was to burn that place to the ground, but rescuing her was most important.

Grace had assured me that this would take a little time, but I was ready to do it come tomorrow.

There was also the fact that I needed to get the book out. The longer it stayed on my computer, *not* accessible by e-readers across the globe, the longer the secret remained behind closed doors.

Part of me thought this feeling self-serving, selfish. The other part was hopeful it would do some good. To prove my intent, I would set the book at $0.99. The royalty I'd make from that would be a pittance, but the book would hopefully have more reach.

But first, as with every good plan, came food. And we could do that at the hotel.

We checked in at the Omni New Haven with ease. After placing an order that had 'already been paid for,' we took a top floor room overlooking Temple Street.

I'd seen this building before, but never thought I'd be staying on the top floor, looking down at the rest of the city. It amazes me to this day the perspectives we gain on our cities, and how quickly they can be turned on their heads by seeing them from a different angle.

As soon as we got in the room, which was a pretty large suite with a nice, comfy bed, I ran to the window to check out our view. I could see West Rock from here, as well as some of Yale's Gothic spires.

"Great view," Grace said as she approached me.

"It is."

She placed her hand on my shoulder. "You want to write."

"Are you telling me to write or reading my mind?"

"You decide."

"I'll write. I need to get this book out, so I can focus on getting Veronique."

I set up my laptop and began editing *Mutants in the Making*. No, I shouldn't have been self-editing my own book, but timing was of the essence, and I had a pretty good AI editor on my laptop that helped out quite a bit.

Luckily, a six-pack of beers came with our food.

To make things simple, we decided on pizza, or as they call it in New Haven, *apizza*. Actually, no one I knew called it that, but at least thinking they called it that made me feel more local even though I was from Rhode Island.

Needless to say, Grace loved the pizza, and I swear she ate six or seven slices.

"When I eat pizza, it reminds me of you," she said as she wolfed down another slice.

Food coma commencing, Grace lay on the bed with a distended belly, and I got back to work.

It was about five o'clock, and I knew I was racing against time. I wanted to go after Veronique tomorrow – tomorrow night to be exact – and I needed this book to be out before we did.

Because I didn't know if we'd be coming back or not.

I formatted the text, made sure the headers looked right, and then I began the long, and tedious, process of using Excel and Paint to create shadow boxes for Grace and Veronique's stats. It was a primitive way to do this; writers now are formatting their characters' stats in a variety of ways, from gifs to advanced Photoshop.

But I was going old school, and everyone who read this book would recognize that.

Street cred, I didn't have much of, but I wanted to have *some* with this book. Besides, it was going to be harder than hell to find readers interested in a creative nonfiction shifter sci-fi story for gamers.

And all of the publishing and editing was a way for me to suppress just how fucked my day had been. I'd seen people die, I'd lost Veronique, and if I didn't already have a target on my ass, I certainly did now.

"Just get the book out," I mumbled to myself as I took a sip of my beer.

I brought up the EBAYmazon direct publishing page, uploaded the cover, uploaded the file, and began working on the product description. Damn did I hate writing product descriptions. That was one of the shitty things about being a self-published author; you had to do all that stuff yourself.

I decided to keep it simple:

A government conspiracy. Secret mutant soldiers. A true story.

What if you were just lying down for bed when a naked woman showed up at your doorstep? What if she was a powerful psychic shifter? What if she had a terrible secret?

Based on a true story, author Gideon Caldwell takes the reader on a journey they won't soon forget. Part one of Mutants in the Making is a living testament to a cover-up that will go on to change the world.

**Superheroes are real, and if we're not careful,
they'll soon become our enemies.**

"What do you think about this?" I asked Grace. I read her the description. "Well?"

"We aren't going to become your enemies," she said after I finished. The lights of the television flashed across her face.

I didn't have to check on her to know that she'd been practicing faces of the people she was watching, mimicking their movements and body posture, then turning back to her base form.

"I know you're not going to become our enemies, but you could. And if you and Veronique truly are super soldiers, then future versions of you could become someone else's enemy. Could be North Korea, or maybe a Middle Eastern country, but still. And Angel? Tell me he's not our enemy."

She shrugged. "I guess that makes sense to me. Can I have a beer?"

Giving a shapeshifter a beer ...?

"Sure, help yourself." I returned to my document.

There was one thing I was forgetting to do.

I pulled the document back up and added a disclaimer to the front and the back. I knew I was going to get some messages from tin hat weirdos, but that came with the territory, and it was something I was willing to sift through.

If you, or anyone you know, has any information about these government experiments, whether it be in America, or another country, please contact Gideon Caldwell at writer_gideon_caldwell@gfacemail.com

With that, I added the disclaimer to the front and back of the book, reuploaded the file, set the price to $0.99 and pressed publish.

My next step was to research as much as I could about the Rose-Lyle Facility. I needed Grace's help for this, so I pulled up a map of Yale campus and had her point out where she'd escaped from.

From there I checked some maps I found on GoogleFace.

Since I had no idea what I was doing, part of my work involved sipping a beer and thinking of the best way to use Grace's abilities to their fullest extent.

One thing was for certain: We weren't going to be able to take Angel head on, not yet anyway. We needed to avoid him altogether, and try to get the hell out of New Haven before he got wind that Veronique was out.

So we definitely needed a getaway car and a plan of escape. Actually, we needed more than one getaway car.

When in doubt, make a list.

I reached for the hotel letterhead and began scratching down some ideas.

Chapter Twenty-One: Ready to Die?

My list of ideas was decent, but there were some factors on it that were going to make them difficult to pull off. For one thing, we needed two vehicles. We also needed a briefcase, a bulletproof vest, some lab coats, money, extra food, and water. I still had no idea how we'd destroy the place, but I'd leave that up to chance a bit. Chance and Veronique …

"Come to bed, Writer Gideon," Grace said as she dropped an empty beer bottle on the ground.

I should have been paying better attention to her, but I was busy formulating my plot.

I could tell by the tone of her voice that she meant business, and besides, who was I to resist her? How could I even resist her? Beauty aside, she could control me. She could control my thoughts, control my actions.

Case in point: I stood up, took my glasses off, and rubbed my eyes. My hands unbuckled my pants on their own accord. I let them fall to the ground as I stepped out of them.

Suddenly, I was back in control.

"I need to take a shower," I told her.

"Hurry," she purred.

I took a beer to the bathroom with me, flicked the shower on, and chugged the beer as I washed my man parts. Nothing worse than stinky man parts. I scrubbed a dub dub, took the last few chugs of my beer, touched the stitches on my face, and carefully washed around the wound.

I'd never had stitches before, and one look in the mirror told me this scar was going to be something that changed people's perceptions of me, like getting a face tattoo.

Also, the bruises on my body were something I didn't expect to see. They lined the inside of my thigh, two were on my arm, and a big one was forming on my shin. The ugly part of having superpowered friends …

Once I finished, I came back into the room with a towel wrapped around my body. I had a feeling I may die the following day; I figured I might as well go out with a bang. And by bang, I mean go out by banging.

Grace sat on the bed in her kimono and geisha form. She looked up at me, her lips pursing into a sexy smile as her robe spilled open.

"Is that how we're going to do it?"

A very small voice at the back of my head screamed that I should be concerned for tomorrow and that I should be shocked about what happened earlier that day, but I silenced that voice.

Or …

I looked at Grace suspiciously.

Yes, Writer Gideon, I'm easing your mind a bit.

I laughed. "Sounds good to me."

She let her kimono spill open even further. I was hypnotized by her dark eyes, the light from the muted TV adding an electric sheen to them.

"Who do you want me to be?" she asked, as her form began to morph.

She was now the spitting image of Natalie Johansson, from the dimples to her thin torso at odds with her bust.

There were a good many men in America whose dream it was to have sex with Natalie Johansson. I never really fantasized about her, but if she showed up at my doorstep and begged me, I wouldn't tell her no.

That got me thinking about who Grace could actually morph into, and I started to wonder if I could possibly have her change into one of my favorite superheroes if I found a good enough picture of them.

Fanboy shit, I know, but I was drunk.

239

"You mean like …" She morphed into Spider Gwen, blonde hair, skintight black and white outfit with a hood. She unzipped the front.

"It's like a cosplay dream," I said as I approached the bed.

From there she turned into Cat Woman, her skin pale, the stitches on her black leather costume barely able to contain her breasts.

"Or would you prefer …?" The top portion of her costume melted and reformed into a tight black military bodysuit. Her facial features elongated, her eyes darkened, and her hair turned blonde and short.

She beckoned me forward with her finger, a faint red energy glowing around her hand.

I gulped. "No, not her."

I didn't know if she turned into Veronique to mess with me, or because she thought it was what I genuinely wanted. Truth be told, I didn't know what I genuinely wanted, but I did know that it pained me to leave Veronique behind.

Grace sensed my hesitation and her skin moved faster than I'd ever seen it move before, quickly reforming her base features.

"Let's keep it simple." She reached for my hand, pulling me in, and I could taste the beer on her breath as we kissed.

She moaned as I moved down her chest to just beneath her belly button. I looked up at her and went to work, my beard tickling against her inner thighs.

I was far from a cunnilingus expert; in fact, it had been a long time since I did something like that. But I gave it my college best – my Southern Connecticut University College best, to be exact – and I don't know if she came or not, but it sure sounded like she did.

After I finished, Grace kicked into high gear, pulling me up, getting on top of me, and gyrating her hips as I slid inside her.

She looked down at me, a smile on her face as her form morphed back to Natalie Johansson, and from there into the newscaster that was on TV at the hotel the other day, then into the Japanese woman, before finally settling back on her base form.

I didn't last long, but it wasn't an endurance game, and I'd already done my fair share by going down on her.

If anything, I would die the following day.

Grace didn't stop me from thinking this as she morphed forms again, this time to one of the maids we'd seen in Stamford and from that to Elektra, her brunette hair long, red corset holding her breasts up.

I threw in the hat at that point.

I had broken bad over the last few days and had finally driven that car off the cliff today, after all the havoc I partially created on the highway.

I was ready for the next day, ready for anything they threw at me, and above all … ready to die.

Of course, when the sun came up the next day I was ready to live. Sore as hell, but ready to seize the day.

I wasn't too familiar with the semi-drunk guy who tried to think like a Bruce Willis archetype after a little sexual healing, but that wasn't who I needed to be at that moment.

You can do it, Gideon! A crowd cheered in my head.

I glanced at Grace to see if she was up. She wasn't, and that only made me feel dumber for cheering myself on.

The first thing I wanted to do was check if *Mutants in the Making* had been published. I stayed in the bed for this, my laptop on my lap as Grace rested next to me.

The book was live, available for the entire world to read.

I then checked the sales ranking. It was somewhere in the mid-millions of the EBAYmazon store, which was utter shit. That meant five million more books were ranked higher than mine.

The odds of my harrowing little tale getting noticed by someone were slim, and decreasing by the hour.

My heart sank.

"There is only one thing in the world worse than being talked about, and that is not being talked about," Oscar Wilde wrote in *The Picture of Dorian Gray.*

Damn, if he wasn't right.

I'd experienced this disappointment several times before and had lifted myself up by the bootstraps once I realized that the book wasn't going to take. It was disheartening, to say the least – akin to gambling, except you were gambling your creativity and losing big. Which was more painful than it seemed.

This book is different, I reminded myself as a sinking feeling in my chest caused my shoulders to droop.

You've created a new genre by publishing it.

After a deep breath in, I refreshed the page to see if there had been any sales or reads.

All EBAYmazon books paid out through either a purchase or by being borrowed and read, even if the reader only read a few pages. Those page reads could add up. Some authors had a hundred thousand page reads a day. I'd be lucky if I had five hundred.

Refreshing the data didn't help any.

I saw that I had sold one of my earlier fantasy works, a book called *How Heavy This Ax,* which was about a transgendered dwarf forced out of his village because of his sexuality.

The Dwarf ends up forming a guild and saving *her* world but is still shunned when *she* comes back to *her* village. Sad story, and a bit experimental. People still seemed to enjoy it though, and by people, I meant that it sold like three to five copies a month. I was particularly proud of the cover.

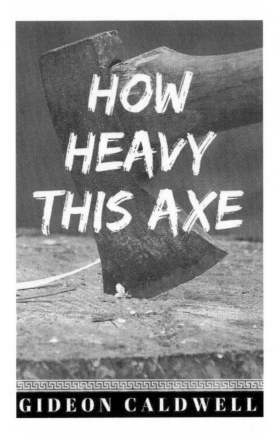

Damn, if that cover didn't take me hours to create.

I told myself that I needed to perk up, to give it time. I'd read about other authors who didn't have success on their launch but came back swinging a few months later.

But you don't have a few months.

For all I knew, I'd be dead by tomorrow.

I hesitated to do some promotions because those were often a crapshoot. I'd wasted thousands of dollars promo-ing books that hardly sold.

Every time I set a promo up, I had this foolish hope it would do something, that I'd get the book in front of the right people and I'd have instant success.

That never turned out to be the case.

As much as I hated to admit it, I probably needed to do some promotion. But I also needed to make preparations for the day.

I got out of bed, slipped my pants on, realized I'd forgotten to put my boxers on, pulled off my pants, put my boxers on, then slipped my pants on again, and looked at my checklist.

"It's a good idea," Grace said from behind me. She had the blanket pulled up to her chest, and her hair was a bit messy, but she looked as striking as ever.

"I didn't think anything ... yet."

Then the idea came to me.

Weird.

"We should definitely find someone to help us, a kind of gopher. Go for this, go for that."

"Like I said, it's a good idea."

Chapter Twenty-Two: Coming Clean to Luke

My phone buzzed, and I looked at it to see a message from Luke.

Luke: Drama in the author community.

Me: Oh?

Luke: One author posted a comment on social media about how this other author's character reminded him of some other author's character, and the author whose character was being referenced got pissed that someone was copying his schtick. So, he said some things in a private message to a friend of the first author, something like that, typical stuff.

Me: Damn, I guess when you get closer to the top there are more people trying to nip at you.

Luke: Speaking of the top, how's your release going?

Me: Not so good.

Luke: Have you hit up your mailing list, or done any promotions yet?

Me: I wish. Actually, my life is taking some pretty strange turns over the last couple of days.

Luke: Does this have anything to do with why you wanted to video chat the other day?

Me: It has everything to do with that.

Luke: Well, do you want to chat now?

Me: I don't know ...

What's there to lose? I had to ask myself. I'd already broken bad and was now being hunted by MercSecure, a quasi-federal agency. *There's nothing left to lose.*

Me: What I'm about to show you is going to freak you out. So be sure you're seated, and that there's no one else around.

Luke: I'm excited!

I turned to Grace. "Hey, I'm going to introduce you to my friend, and I want you to show him your abilities."

She sat up, her breasts now resting over the edge of the blanket.

"And, um, you'll probably want to put some clothes on too."

My sweater appeared on her body. I still did not understand how that worked, and I didn't think I ever would. That's the thing about shifters – at some point you just learn to accept them and not question how it is they are able to do what they do.

I pressed the video chat button and it quickly connected.

"You've got a beard too," Luke said just as his image appeared on my screen. He also had a beard, but his was much lighter than mine. His eyes were dark, his cheeks were a little red, and his lips looked chapped.

"I'm about to tell you a lot of things," I said. "Things you may not believe until I show you evidence of what's happened to me."

Concern grew on his face. "Is everything all right, buddy? And what happened to your face? Where did you get that cut? Didn't know you shaved your head."

I settled my thoughts and started from the top. I told him about Grace's sudden appearance and her abilities; I told him about the men in black; I told him about plugging into Grace's neck and when we were first attacked by Veronique; I told him about Veronique's abilities, and how she kidnapped me and threatened to kill me; then I told him about the attack at the hotel back in Stamford and about Angel; I explained what I planned to do next and how my book relayed all this information, aside from the very last bit about Angel, because that would be in the second installment.

Luke laughed nervously, a hint of skepticism in his eyes. "That's a pretty crazy story."

"And it's a true story. Now I present my evidence. Grace," I turned my phone's camera to her, "say hi to Luke."

Grace crawled on the bed over to me and sat on its corner. She looked at the phone for a moment and then smiled at Luke.

"So, this is Grace?" Luke asked. I could no longer see his face, so I didn't know how he was reacting to meeting her.

"Hi, Luke," Grace said.

"Hi!"

I nodded at Grace, and her face began to morph into Luke's, from his auburn hair down to his chapped lips.

"Holy shit!" came his voice from the phone's little speaker. "Shit! Shit! Shit!"

"Change into something else," I instructed her.

Her form began to change into the cute redhead with freckles, the same form she'd taken when we first checked into the hotel in East Haven.

"No way."

Still keeping the front of the phone faced at Grace, I backed away a bit so he could see the full effect.

"Stand up," I told her, "and change into the first thing that comes to your mind."

She changed into a stunningly beautiful black woman, with an afro parted down the middle, waist-high shorts, and long, sleek legs.

"This cannot be real, this cannot be real."

Her next form was that of a man, the trucker who died getting us to New Haven. She was now short, stout, her belly hanging over her waist, warts on her face, and stringy hair sticking out of a hat with a fishing hook on its brim.

Finally, she took her base form, my sweater and loose pants forming on her body.

"Gideon, let me see you now," Luke said.

I turned the phone back to my face. I wasn't smiling; this wasn't me trying to show off. I was relieved to finally share my secret, but sharing it didn't make me happy, it only made me realize yet again the crazy shit I'd gotten my ass into.

"Damn, man, so your book *is* true," Luke finally said after a few seconds of silence. "You weren't lying to me."

"I hate to say it, man, but I don't think I could make this shit up."

"I cannot believe ... No, I saw it with my own two eyes. It's true. It's just ... You can't go viral with this."

"I wasn't planning to. I wanted to put the writing out there, with the hopes of finding more information about people who have been experimented on and where they are. It's not my intention to create some type of media circus about this."

Luke looked at me incredulously. "But if the book reaches enough people, it *will* create a media circus."

"Well, fuck, you're right about that. I already have sort of a disguise going on with my shaved head, beard, and scar – or future scar, since it's still healing. For Grace, it'll be easy, but for Veronique …"

"And now you're going after her, correct? You're going after her tonight, you said."

"I am. And I don't care if I die in the process. I know that sounds crazy, but I think this is worth it and that I share the story with you, and the book is out there. What will be, will be."

If I sounded confident saying that, I sure didn't feel confident saying it. I swallowed hard, steadying my gaze on Luke.

He nodded. "I've got a few friends who have a pretty big reach on the web, and they owe me some favors. I'm going to do what I can to help you get your book in their spheres. I don't know if I'll ever see you again after tonight, and just for the record, I don't think you should do what you're planning to do. As cool as it sounds, this is real life. You are not a superhero, and just because you have somehow surrounded yourself with them, doesn't mean you should go out kicking down the doors of government agencies. It's lunacy."

I took a deep and steady breath. He was right, completely right, and what I was planning to do was crazy. "I know, and I appreciate the sentiment. But it's where my life is at, and it's what needs to be done."

"Understood, and please, contact me as soon as you are safe. If you don't contact me, I'm going to assume the worst. I'll do what I can to spread the information about what has happened to you. The book too. I'll read it today. I want to catch up with what's going on. I don't know how much I can help you, but I'll try."

"Thank you," I said. "Truly, thank you. And about tonight … let's just see if our plan works."

He gave me a toothy grin. "Gideon Caldwell, if this is the last time I meet you, it was nice knowing you, and you are one crazy motherfucker. I'm glad to call you my friend. And I wish there was more I could do, aside from trying to help you get your book out."

"Thanks, man."

"Tell Grace I said goodbye."

"Bye, Writer Luke," Grace called over to him.

"Let's get to breakfast, and see what we can discover down there," I told Grace after I hung up the phone. Confession had taken a terrible burden off my shoulders, and I could see how it was used as a way to relieve people.

It really helped to talk about these things, but without evidence, I don't think he would have bought it.

Hell, *I* wouldn't have believed me.

"I was going to suggest that."

I gave her a funny look.

I had the sense that she was putting thoughts in my mind, but then again, maybe I was thinking my own thoughts. But this was only the start of the problem. It would always be hard for me to tell if I was the one thinking something, or if Grace was thinking something for me.

We would become increasingly symbiotic in that way.

Breakfast at the Omni was decent, and there was no waffle machine, so I had to suffice with potatoes, eggs, cinnamon rolls, cereal, and bagel, all of which were delicious. I sat in front of Grace, sipping coffee, when I saw just who I was looking for.

"That's our guy," I whispered as a businessman sat down across from us, with a pretty hefty briefcase in tow. I didn't know why he had such a large briefcase, but it would come in handy for what needed to be done later that day.

Grace turned to look at him, and as soon as they locked eyes, he pushed his chair back, stood up, and came over to our table.

"Do you mind if I join you?" he asked.

"By all means," I said with a grin.

"My name's Chip Parker." He smiled crookedly at me. He was in his forties, and the business card he gave me indicated he was a regional manager at a project management company. He was fit, bald, and had bushy black eyebrows.

"What would you like Chip to do first?" Grace asked me.

I was nervous about all this, but that nervousness was considerably less than the nervousness I'd felt a few days ago. I was hardening, toughening up, and as I pulled my list out of my back pocket, I tried to look as nonchalant and confident as possible.

You have this, Gideon, Grace's voice whispered in my head.

"The first thing we need is your briefcase, Chip," I told him.

He set his briefcase on the table, popped it open, and began taking his iPad and all the papers out.

"Do you have a car with you?"

"Just a rental," he told me.

"Put your stuff back in the briefcase and take it to your rental car. Put all of your belongings in the trunk, and bring the briefcase back to us."

"Sure thing."

It felt strange to be able to tell someone to do something like that. For a split second, I thought that maybe I had psychic abilities, but the reality of our situation washed over me like the Cold Bucket Challenge. It was all Grace's doing.

The thought that I may have a super ability reminded me of finding my picture on Grace's drive.

"It's not what you think it is," she said as we waited for Chip.

I knew in my heart I wasn't a superpowered individual. It was clear; I'd never remotely exhibited anything that would have made me think I had some type of power or sway over the natural environment.

I'd never accidentally lifted something with my mind; I'd never blasted someone with a fireball that appeared spontaneously in the palm of my hand; and I clearly did not have healing capabilities, as evidenced by the future scar on my face.

"Later," she told me. "We'll deal with that later."

Chip returned with an empty briefcase. "How's this, boss?" he asked me.

"Boss?" I looked at Grace.

"I thought you'd like that touch."

"Chip, we're going to need your help today. Please, sit."

He coughed in his hand and took a seat before me.

"The first thing I want you to do is to go get a bunch of healthy snacks and bottles of water. I also want you to go to a military surplus store and get a bulletproof vest, and possibly one of those assault team helmets. There may not be one of those stores here in New Haven, so you might have to go to Bridgeport or possibly even Hartford. You know what I mean. I need two lab coats, and two sets of scrubs – one for a male and one for a female. Also, get me a backpack."

"Great – so food, medical clothes, backpack, and a vest. Is there a particular way I should pay?"

"That part doesn't matter to me. Just pay with whatever you have, put this stuff in your trunk, and bring it back here. You're going to be our driver tonight. And tomorrow, you're not going to remember any of this."

"Okay, should I steal a car for you? Or would you like to borrow my car?"

I pinched the bridge of my nose. "We'll get the cars. I know how much of a pain it can be dealing with rental car insurance companies. Don't worry about the vehicles."

"Sounds good," he said, his bushy brows pressing together as he nodded at me.

"Grace and I have a few errands we need to run, but we plan to meet you back here in a couple of hours. What room are you in?"

"Room 301."

"Great, once you finish gathering the supplies, I want you to go back to your room and wait for us there. Do not take any calls, do not watch any TV, and do not use the internet. Just relax. Got it?"

Chip stood and offered us a curt little nod. "I'll see you two later."

Chapter Twenty-Three: Cherry Blossoms Revisited

It didn't take us very long to find our first vehicle. As soon as we left the Omni New Haven, we saw a nature-y looking guy get out of his Toyota Tacoma to pay a parking meter. Grace approached him. He realized that the Tacoma 'wasn't his truck' and readily handed me the keys.

"Tell him he sold his truck and that he decided to take up biking."

"That's a great idea," the man said almost instantly. "I think I'll take up biking."

We needed to get to a place where there was money, which would likely be parts of Hamden or Orange, two smaller cities not far from New Haven. Hamden was closer, so I drove the Tacoma there first.

I took Whitney Avenue, went the back way so we'd come out near the Stop and Shop and found our target. I parked in the lot of a Bank of America, and we waited for people to pull up in their cars.

Grace was able to access someone's memories just by seeing them, and doing so allowed her to quickly decipher if they were wealthy or not.

So, as a warm breeze blew up from the south, whipping at a discarded McStarbucks bag, we waited for our marks to arrive.

Anyone who was wealthy was called over to the truck, where I did the talking, and Grace did the rest.

"I need you to get the ten thousand dollars you owe me," I told an older woman with a Louis Vuitton bag. "Get it in cash. Just bring it back here and we'll call it even."

It was surprisingly easy.

The people would go in the bank, come back with cash, give it to us and leave, their memories scrubbed by Grace.

Thirty minutes later, we'd accumulated about forty grand, no small feat.

For a disguise, Grace had morphed into a brunette in a hoodie with yoga pants and a pair of sunglasses. She looked hot, mysterious … like she could be the lead female in the next *Transformers* installment. I was in my Yale cap and sunglasses – a creeper if there ever was one, but definitely incognito.

With forty thousand in the glove compartment, we changed locations, taking the highway to Orange, Connecticut, where we found a Wells Fargo set in a building that must have been built in the seventies.

We only managed to get ten thousand out of this one before a security guy started poking around. Of course, Grace could have done something to him, but he may have had a body cam, and I didn't want anything to be on a camera.

So we moved on.

We now had fifty thousand dollars *cash*, something I never even dreamed of holding before. But we needed more, and I wanted to make sure there was enough to cover us for a while just in case we had to barter.

Sure, Grace's ability was on our side, but a little cash money never hurt anyone.

It only took us a moment driving down Boston Post Road to find another bank, this time of Chase, where we netted thirty thousand.

Eighty grand should definitely be enough to tide us over for a bit, I thought as I merged back onto the highway.

Even though I was feeling tough, and even though a very childish part of me wanted to fan myself with the money or make it rain like I was in a rap video, I was completely terrified.

I had to keep reminding myself that I'd broken bad. In a big way.

But it wasn't as easy as it sounded, and it got me thinking about all those who had broken bad. How did they sleep at night?

This is your life until you're either caught ...

Or else.

"Quiet, Writer Gideon," Grace said. "And take me back to the cherry blossoms."

I thought about this for a moment. Wooster Square wasn't far from our hotel, and we could simply circle the square if we thought something looked suspicious.

"Yeah, let's go there."

We took the exit on I-95 that passed by the dozen Latin American food trucks set up along the wharf. Then a left under the highway, and we drove in front of Ikea and that weird building that had been erected before it – some concrete monstrosity from a forgotten age.

We got to Wooster Square, and once I saw that the coast was clear and there weren't any quasi-federal agent types poking around, I parked the truck.

"Let's make it quick," I told her. "And let's try to stay near the truck, just in case."

"You worry too much," she said with a soft, yet comical smile. She bent forward, kissed me, and got out of the truck.

Feeling emboldened, I got out too, and I didn't even pay the meter. I wasn't planning to be there for very long anyway.

The cherry blossoms that line the street still had a few more days left before their petals would start falling. Grace was in heaven, moving toward the trees, her arms spread wide as she spun and looked up at the blossoms. She never seemed happier than when she saw those trees.

Maybe they represented something else to her … the first taste of freedom, perhaps.

After all, they were the first thing she saw of the real world (if you don't count my street on a dark and stormy night or my less than comfy basement apartment). Just standing near the square brought back a series of memories. The pizza restaurants had already fired up their ovens, and there were a few people in the center of the square, walking their dogs and living the good life.

"Are there cherry blossoms where we're going next?" she asked me.

I hadn't decided yet where we were going next, but I knew it was somewhere other than Connecticut, and definitely not New Haven. "You know, I have no idea," I told her. "But wherever we're going, there will be pretty flowers."

"I don't know if there are prettier flowers than these." She reached up to one of the trees and pulled down a cherry blossom. Grace sniffed it, laughed a little when she saw the look I was giving her, and threw it over her shoulder.

"You didn't have to stop," I told her. "I was admiring you."

"Uh-huh."

Not really an answer, but that was fine. It was really nice just to see her happy, and to realize that this brief little interlude, our walk through the cherry blossoms, really brought her so much joy.

We took a quick walk around the square, and I couldn't help but feel nervous the entire time. Even after she spoke inside my head, I still felt that familiar tension in my chest, a tension telling me that we were being watched and that they may come for us at any time.

No matter how many deep breaths I took, the sensation always returned. It would be a feeling that would come to define my life for the next few weeks and months.

After we left Wooster Square, I gassed up the Tacoma, paying in cash, and we returned to the hotel's underground parking lot.

Everything was going according to plan.

We called the cab with an actual driver – no AI this time – and he arrived about six minutes later.

Our cabbie was a Puerto Rican guy with a pair of thick black sunglasses on and a cross tattoo on the side of his neck. He seemed pretty laid back, but of course, I would never know his true personality due to the fact that Grace had already taken over his mind just about as quickly as it took someone to blink.

"Take us to Hamden," I told him as I got in. "Drive us around one of those fancy neighborhoods."

"You got it, amigo."

We cut down Whitney Avenue, Yale on our left and right, as we took the back way to Hamden. Or maybe it was the front way.

At any rate, it felt kind of odd to be driving through Yale with the notion that we'd be assaulting one of their facilities later. Then again, if all the well-dressed students walking around only knew the kind of shit their university was getting into …

But all that could be exposed later.

I mentioned the fact that it was Yale University in *Mutants in the Making*, and if the book got popular enough, I was sure Yale would release some statement denying it. But like most denials released by governments, corporations, and universities, there was usually more than an ounce of truth to what they were discrediting.

To the richer neighborhoods we go! I thought, switching my inner musings over to the fact that our plan was coming to fruition.

"Only one more car to go," I said excitedly.

"A convertible?" Grace asked.

"We'll see."

We took a left on Mathis Avenue and drove around aimlessly, looking for the right vehicle. After about five minutes, I spotted a brand new Dodge Charger parked in front of a large white house with a nice picket fence and a fancy veranda. The Charger was black, fierce, and the way it was shaped reminded me of a panther about to strike.

"That's the one," I told our driver. "Wait here until we get our vehicle; once we get it, you're free to go, sir."

I reached into my pocket and pulled out a wad of cash, I counted out a thousand bucks and stuffed it in the front pocket of his T-shirt, instructing him not to look at it until later.

"You got it," he said with a smile.

Hopefully the owner is home, I thought as Grace and I walked to the front door.

"I have a feeling he or she may be," Grace said. I knew she couldn't tell the future per se, but I did get an uneasy feeling about the way she said that.

We knocked on the door, waited, knocked again, and on the final knock, a man opened the door, hastily covering his body with a robe. He was in his thirties and fit, with a lantern jaw and a full head of hair.

"Ah, he's cheating on his wife right now," Grace said, her eyes turning white.

"Good to know," I mumbled under my breath.

"How can I help you?" he asked. "Would you like the keys to my car?"

"Yeah, that would be nice," I told him. "Give me the keys to your car, and then go back to doing whatever it is you were doing in there. If anyone asks you about the car, I want you to say you let your friend borrow it. I also want you to delete any information you have on its VIN number or license plate number."

"Got it," he said, turning away from the door.

I had to remind myself that I wasn't the one who was a psychic, but it sure as hell felt like it. The better Grace and I got at tag-teaming our marks, the more it felt like I too had a superpower. Later I'd have to constantly remind myself that I didn't have any powers and that I was just a normal guy.

But it felt pretty cool in the moment. And the tiny voice at the back of my head told me we should go to Vegas if we got the chance.

The cheating man returned a few moments later with his wallet and a woman on his arm. She was also in her thirties, heavier than him, with nice features and light hazel eyes.

"What's the meaning of this?" she asked, but by the time she got the last word out, Grace had taken over.

266

The woman just smiled at us as the man dropped the keys into my hand.

I started speaking again. "I want both of you to forget about this car. You've never seen this car, you never bought this car, and you're going to spend weeks trying to figure out why people keep telling you that you have a car when you don't."

"Sounds like it'll be challenging," he said. "But I'm always up for a challenge."

"That's the spirit," I told him, a bit surprised by his answer.

I thanked the man and the woman, wished them luck in their adultery, and as we turned to leave, I waved at the cab driver.

He took off, and Grace and I got into the Dodge Charger.

Boy, was it a beast.

As soon as my foot hit the gas pedal we were off, tires peeling out as we hit the hard streets of Hamden, Connecticut.

I sped up to a stop sign only to slam on the brakes.

"Wow!" Grace laughed.

"Just testing them," I told her, feeling like an utter badass.

I fishtailed a bit as I got used to the feel of the vehicle. The dashboard was the exact opposite of the BMW we'd stolen a few days back. It was fierce, aggressive, and masculine, and I noticed that I could turn on auto drive with a simple flick of a switch.

Not bad.

We fueled up, returned to the hotel, and drove into the Omni garage, parking a few spots down from our Tacoma. I could now check 'two cars' off my list.

We found Chip Parker in his room on the third floor. He stood once we entered and greeted us. "The trunk is filled with food, as you requested. I've got the bulletproof vest, a ballistic full-face helmet, and the medical clothes."

"Let me see the vest."

The body armor was as I expected, the helmet something else entirely. It was black, with straps that went around my chin, and an attached piece that covered my face, still allowing me to see but adding just a little bit more protection from debris.

I wasn't stupid enough to think it could take a shot, but if someone like Angel decided to punch through a wall next to me, it would help.

"The scrubs and lab coats are in the backpack," he told me.

"Great," I said as I tried the vest on. It fit perfectly. "You've done an excellent job," I told him. "There's only a few more things to do."

"What's that?" he asked, his bushy eyebrows lifting.

He listened intently as I explained the next step.

"Great, I'll get right on that. Do you want me to return here after I finish?"

"Sure, come back here, or meet us at our room on the top floor."

You need to give him your duffle bag and laptop to put in the Dodge.

I smiled at Grace; she was right.

"Actually, come up with us to our room so I can give you some stuff to take to the Dodge."

"Got it."

Chip packed up all of our stuff and followed us up to our room. I quickly tossed the clothes I'd left on the floor into the duffle bag, followed by my laptop and Yale hat. I needed to get rid of that damn hat, but it was what I had at the moment.

"This is it," I told Chip. I handed him the bag, the keys, and off he went.

Grace yawned. "Want to rest before we begin?"

I smiled at her as she changed back into her base form, her hair growing long, her features lightening, her eyes turning a crisp blue.

"Definitely. I want to eat something too."

"How about pizza?"

"You smelled it earlier too? In Wooster Square?"

"It's so good," she said, licking her lips.

"Sure, Grace, let's get a pizza."

What a fitting choice for what may be my last meal on Earth, I thought as I sat in a chair near the window.

Chapter Twenty-Four: Easy Access

I asked Grace to lie down on the bed so I could play with her stats for a moment. I had a feeling there was more I would be able to do with them, but I wasn't quite as computer savvy as others, and there was a lot of information in her system that made no sense to me.

I logged in, the shadow box came up, and I began looking through files. I wasn't able to locate the picture of myself, a conundrum that still burned at the back of my mind.

Had I been part of these experiments?

The answer to that would anger me, but it would still be some time before I learned the truth.

Not able to really sleuth anything out, I moved to her psychic abilities.

Main: Psychic

Omnikinesis: 10

Second Sight: 5

Psychometry: 5

Telepathy: 6

Clairsentience: 5

Psychokinesis: 7

Hypnosis: 5

I wished I could crank up Omnikinesis to eleven a la *Spinal Tap,* but ten was the best I could do; the dial wouldn't go any higher. I moved to her second ability.

Main Second: Shifter

Speed of Change: 10

Texture Consistency: 10

Opacity: 10

Voice Match: 10

One good thing about her morphing ability was that changing any of the numbers didn't alter the others.

I decided to play around with what was listed though and turned the texture consistency down to one.

As I did, the hooded sweatshirt and yoga pants she wore turned shiny, as if they'd been spray painted on. I reached out and touched her leg, noticing that it felt more or less like skin now, even though she technically had a pair of pants on. And no, that wasn't a dig on yoga pants and how tight they'd become by 2030 – it legitimately felt like skin.

"Change to a sweater," I told her.

My sweater took shape on her body – the same one I'd given her back at my place – only now it seemed like it had been painted it on somehow. There was no texture to it, and I could see in detail the contours of her body and her nipples beneath it.

So, texture consistency does exactly what I thought it did. Duh. I turned it back up to ten, the wool and fuzz on my sweater reappeared, and I moved on to opacity.

This was what we would use later tonight. I turned it down, and as I did, she began to fade away. I could sense if she moved – thank you, reptilian brain! – even though she was now completely see-through.

I turned the dial back to ten.

"This will work," I told her. "But I'd really like to see some building schematics."

"They're in there," she said, and suddenly, I felt as if Grace had possessed me.

She still lay in front of me, but fuzziness clouded my psyche, and my hand began to scroll through her drive *on its own.*

The folders opened, as did subfolders, and more subfolders. Eventually, she pulled up the Rose-Lyle building schematics and downloaded them onto my smartphone. I was a silent observer in all this, my actions far from my own.

I started to get the weird sense that Grace knew everything, that she was some type of goddess, and it was only when she chuckled that I realized she'd left my head.

"What?" I asked her.

"I'm no goddess," she said.

"I don't know how amplified your power can become," I admitted, "but you could end up as a goddess at the rate you're going. What you just did was phenomenal. Everything you do defies explanation."

She frowned at this.

"What?"

"Sometimes I just want to be normal."

I didn't say anything, letting that comment just simmer for a bit.

I was about to pull up the map and figure out the best way forward when I noticed another file had downloaded onto my phone. I clicked on it, and the PDF quickly loaded. It was a schematic for the plug that was installed in Grace's neck. Parts of it were too technical, but it did show basic design and installation instructions.

I saved this as well.

"You don't happen to know where the cameras are, do you?" I asked after I opened the map on my phone.

"No."

"We'll have to be hyper-aware of cameras."

I could tell by the schematics that there was an odd, square-shaped room only accessible after a long hallway, well past the basement. The room was listed as the 'Plastic Room,' a clear indication that it would be the right place to store someone with Veronique's abilities.

There were restrooms outside the entrance to this room, which would be a great place for me to hole up while Grace did her thing. I knew I was of no help, aside from being able to turn her invisible, so my job would be to wait for her to come back with Veronique. Besides, we'd be able to communicate telepathically.

We got a call from the front desk that the pizza had arrived.

"You want me to get it?" Grace asked as I unplugged from her neck.

"No, I have cash."

Chip Parker sat in the driver's seat, Grace next to him in a lab coat and scrubs. I was next to her, also dressed like a doctor. I wore the bulletproof vest under my lab coat and had placed the ballistics helmet and the other pair of scrubs in the backpack, which was stuffed between my legs.

Grace's scrubs, of course, had been made on her own volition. The set in my backpack was for Veronique.

It was night now, and a light fog had settled over the city of New Haven. The streets were relatively empty, lit by dim orange lights.

We pulled into a parking lot less than a block away from the entrance to the Rose-Lyle facility. It amazed me that they'd done all this experimental work so close to the campus center, with its old brick buildings reminiscent of Colonial America.

"We'll be back," I told Chip.

"I'll be waiting," he said, his eyes locked on the dashboard.

Weird.

Whatever happened to us, I wanted to make sure Chip got some money for his troubles, so I stuck a roll of hundred-dollar bills in his hand and told him to reimburse himself for his expenses.

"Will do," he said, eyes still locked on the dashboard.

"You ready?" I asked Grace as I got out of the truck. This time she had gone for an Asian man with unkempt hair, rimless glasses, and a mad scientist look about him.

She nodded, and I asked her to lead the way.

277

We walked like colleagues, my backpack slung over one shoulder like I was a graduate student. With my glasses, shaggy beard, and doctorly outfit, I looked a little unorthodox, but definitely not out of place, which was exactly what I was going for.

I followed Grace through a checkpoint and an armed guard waved us in after verifying our credentials.

My 'credentials' were little more than a Krunkin' Kronuts card my uncle had given me. Grace didn't have a card at all, so the guard examined mine again, scanned it – it came back false – and let us through.

With that, we were in. We hung to the left as we entered a long corridor with hallways jutting off rhizomatically. I briefly glanced at my phone to make sure we were going in the right direction.

Once I confirmed this, we headed deeper into the facility until we got to an elevator. There were other scientists around, and a few places that didn't seem as restricted as others, but the elevator was clearly marked for restricted access only.

This presented a problem, as we didn't have a badge to scan us in. We waited for a few nervous minutes as I kept expecting whatever security apparatus patrolled the facility to come around the corner and hold us up.

Eventually, an Indian scientist stepped out of the elevator, *and directly into Grace's trap.*

One glance at him and he turned back to the elevator, scanned us in, and went to the basement with us.

Who knew all this was down here? I thought as we entered a room that was almost like a subway platform. We got into a metal pod and the doors locked into place. The pod took off with the three of us inside, and as it did, I traced its trajectory on my phone's map.

What I had thought was a long corridor, was actually some type of hyperloop tunnel.

It didn't take us very long to get to the other end, and after the pod slowed to a halt, we stepped out onto a wide platform with a single door at its apex. We entered a much narrower hallway, turned a corner, and I froze.

There was a moving camera on the wall currently aimed directly at us. Grace and I pretended to talk to each other, and once the camera rotated in the other direction, we slipped into the restroom.

The Indian man now stood in front of the bathroom door, his hands on his hips as he awaited instruction.

"Do you have access to the Plastic Room?" I asked him point-blank.

"I do."

After double-checking to make sure there weren't any cameras in the bathroom – there weren't – I plugged into Grace's neck and found her opacity setting.

279

"Remember, let me know what's going on by communicating here," I said, touching my head.

I could no longer see her, but when she moved to the door, I caught a slight hint of her body. The Indian man followed her out.

I took my place in a stall and put the ballistic helmet on. And as stupid as it was, I took a picture of myself and sent it to Luke, figuring it may be the last picture I ever sent out.

Luke: Holy shit! Are you serious right now?

Me: Just in case I don't make it out. We've arrived and are rescuing V as we speak.

Luke: 😮 *Keep me up to date, buddy. Please, be safe! I've never had to tell someone 'don't get shot' but ...*

Me: That's what the vest and the helmet are for.

Luke: You look like Shredder, or Snake Eyes, or Snake Eyes meets Shredder. It's a good look, but seriously, oh my god, Gideon! Good luck. Seriously, good fucking luck!

Chapter Twenty-Five: The Plastic Room

We are in and moving toward the Plastic Room.

Great, I thought back to her. I was still in the bathroom stall furthest from the door pretending to be going number two just in case someone came in.

Talk about on edge.

If I had any nails left to bite I would have bitten them clean off. I was panicked, my mouth was dry, and my breaths were shallow. This was it, if we got Veronique and made it out of here, we'd get out alive. Hopefully. A proverbial cleanup crew could also be on their way, and we'd be trapped far beneath the city of New Haven.

This begged the question: *What if they find you in here?*

I didn't even want to think what would happen if they found me in the bathroom.

Relax, Writer Gideon.

I had to smile. Just hearing Grace's sweet voice in my head cooled my nerves. That was, until someone came into the bathroom to take a piss. He was a heavy-footed fellow, a little gassy too. The guy grunted as his stream hit the porcelain, and after a long sigh, he was gone.

Someone may be coming your way, I thought to Grace.

No matter.

That last phrase from her left me feeling a bit uneasy. What was she going to do?

Omnikinesis, I reminded myself.

That's right.

I cracked a grin. She really was something else. As I sat on the toilet waiting for destiny to take its toll, a quote from *Dune* came to me: "The mystery of life isn't a problem to solve, but a reality to experience."

I suppose Frank Herbert was right, but then again, he'd never broken bad like I had. I mean, having people battle over spice is one thing, but finding yourself in an underground facility …

Ha! You're an idiot.

I needed another term aside from 'break bad,' but damn if it didn't fit. From a shitty sci-fi writer who worked at a gift shop to the resistance.

Yeah, the resistance.

I tried to quiet my mind and failed. I began counting back from one hundred, hoping that would help some. It didn't. I then tried to focus on the gunmetal gray of the bathroom stall, and from there to the halogen lamp above, and then to the stall door, noticing that it had recently been repaired, as evidenced by the newness of the screws.

"Quiet, Writer Gideon," I mumbled to myself. Pranayama breaths, going over the map, trying to remember everything that had happened over the last days – I still couldn't calm my mind.

My spirit nearly left my body when the bathroom door kicked open and Grace whispered my name.

I burst out of the stall to find the Indian scientist and another guy holding up Veronique, who was wearing a hospital gown. Her head was bent forward, she was breathing hard, her blonde hair was tangled, and the look in her eyes was one of utter madness.

As the two men stared at me, their eyes completely white, Veronique's hands landed on their necks. They twitched as she began to consume their power.

"Gideon," Grace said, startling me. I'd forgotten she was invisible. I fumbled to get my phone out to plug back into her port. Once I had the cable ready, she guided it into the port for me.

I started the system, pulled up the abilities menu, and adjusted her opacity.

She reverted back to her Asian scientist form just as the two men behind her fell. Veronique crouched over them, continuing to consume their life force. Her skin was glowing, the look on her face predatory, but something about the way she held herself told me she was still weak.

Even after feeding on two people?

The men's bodies shriveled until they resembled prunes. Rather than feel disgusted at the gruesome sight, I ignored it and got the scrubs out. Together, Grace and I began dressing Veronique, who was still pretty loopy.

"What did they do to you?"

Sorrow appeared in the corners of her dark eyes.

"It doesn't matter," I told her. "We're here now."

She let us take her shirt off and place the scrub over her body. To get the pants on, I lifted her and placed her on the counter, careful to avoid a small puddle of water.

I pulled her pants on and her arms draped around my shoulders. She started to sob, stopped immediately and took a deep breath, then made sure her pants were on completely.

"We're almost out of here," I told her. "Stay with me now."

I did not think about footwear, but then again, these disguises were only to make it a bit harder to spot us from a distance. Grace would be able to handle anyone who was in our immediate vicinity.

I cupped Veronique's face in my hands. "Are you strong enough?"

"I need more," she whispered, her throat parched. "More."

I glanced at Grace and she nodded. "Do it, Writer Gideon."

"Use me," I told Veronique, my hands still on her face. "Just let me have enough energy to be able to walk."

She swallowed hard as her hand lifted to my arm, red energy radiating from her fingertips.

I grew woozy.

My knees started to buckle and as they did, she let up.

Grace moved forward to catch me as I started to fall. Veronique quickly joined her in holding me up.

"Thank you." She guided me to the sink so I could brace my hands on it for support. "I think they have just a little more."

Veronique knelt by the first scientist, the Indian guy, and finished him off. She then moved to the second, her hand on the guy's forehead as his skin turned the color of a plum.

"Are you good?" I asked, my voice cracking.

"Much better than before."

Grace stepped out to make sure the camera was not facing us – not that it mattered at that point – and we left the bathroom. After traveling through a few hallways, we arrived in the room that reminded me of a subway platform and took the hyperloop pod to the main facility.

It was one of the longest rides of my life, even though it would finish in about a minute.

Whatever lay in the main body of the Rose-Lyle facility could be our undoing. We'd made it this far, but I had a feeling things were about to get a lot worse.

I stayed down, my ballistics helmet now on my head, front piece covering my face. I was braced, willing and ready for shit to hit the fan once the pod doors opened.

Grace was standing, poised to use her abilities, her eyes flaring white. Veronique stood as well, her fists at her sides as the pod slowed to a halt.

The two exchanged glances as the pod doors hissed opened.

I let out a sigh loud enough for all of us. It startled Veronique. Grace laughed a little and offered me a slight grin.

There was no one waiting for us.

"What?" I asked. "This is tense!"

After gathering our nerves, we exited the pod and used the scientist's keycard to take the elevator up to the top.

Grace and Veronique went out at the same time, and both found themselves in an empty hallway. I came out next, looking like the ultra noob in my lab coat, backpack, bulletproof vest, and futuristic ballistic helmet.

Where the hell is everyone?

I knew my way to the exit – I was good with direction like that – and after we waited another moment to see if something would happen, we continued forward.

No one was around, and the cameras on the wall didn't follow us as we passed, which was odd.

They are planning something, either Grace said in my head, or I thought.

"I know they are."

Veronique looked at me curiously. "Know what?"

I don't speak in her head.

"Grace and I think they're planning something."

Veronique looked at us like we were amateurs. "It took you this long to come to that conclusion? You guys just break in here and take me out, and you don't think they're going to be waiting? They are going to be waiting."

My heart sank. "I know, you're right." I cleared my throat. "We have to push forward."

We cleared the main hall and arrived at the front entrance. Everything was still, from the security cameras to the fake plants in the corner.

Veronique looked back at me. "Are you two ready?"

Grace nodded.

"Ready as I'll ever be," I said, still feeling weak.

We pushed the door open and a giant spotlight flashed on.

We were surrounded by men in black paramilitary outfits pointing assault rifles at us. Before Veronique could turn their weapons on them, one of the men bolted up into the air and slammed down next to her, sending the three of us flying in his wake.

There was only one man I'd ever seen move that quickly. Before I could even get to my feet, Angel grabbed me by the throat and lifted me into the air.

Chapter Twenty-Six: Calling Angel Out

The world fell away as Angel carried me higher into the sky. I struggled to free myself, but I was weak, and the sound of bullets firing at Grace and Veronique was too much for me to handle.

New Haven and the rest of Yale looked so far away now, just lights below, no different than the lights above.

I was delirious, gravity was doing all sorts of shit to my body, and it was only when we began to fall back to the earth that I started to scream.

Angel curved up just in time and we landed on the rooftop.

His hand still around my neck, he pulled back and threw me into an air conditioning unit. The impact made me taste blood and it knocked the air out of me. My ballistics helmet was still on my head, strapped under my chin, and I could feel the warm metal pressed into the sweat of my face.

I tried to get back on my knees, but Angel approached me and picked me up again by the throat. With his other hand, he tore off the bottom portion of my helmet, removing the cover over my jaw.

"Anything you'd like to say before I do what I should have done yesterday?" he asked me. A few strands of his long black hair fell into his face.

It took all I had, but I forced the word out. "Why?"

He lifted me a bit higher.

If he had wanted to, he could have easily broken my back using the corner of the air conditioning unit. He could have thrown me off the roof or given me the Bane treatment, snapping me over his leg like cracking a stick.

Instead, he lowered me ever so slightly.

"What do you mean by why?"

"Why are you working for them?" I asked. "Didn't they make you the same way they made Veronique and Grace, I mean Sabine? Aren't you a super soldier they created? Won't they retire you to create a better version?"

"I believe that is an option we all face. There isn't a human on this Earth who isn't a stone's throw away from being replaced by something new."

A gust of wind lashed at his long brown hair and his grip loosened. I fell to the ground.

"What's your name?" he asked me, menacingly.

"Gideon."

"Hmmm …" He glanced up at the stars, then back down at me. "You will die here tonight, Gideon, yet you wonder about me and my future. How very odd of you."

"I just wanted to know why you would do this to someone who's trying to help. I just want to be honest with you."

"Trying to help me?" He laughed bitterly. "You are one of them."

"What's that supposed to mean?"

I was starting to get my breath back and was surprised to find I could actually speak. That's not to say I wasn't completely petrified by the man who stood before me, and his ability to stop me as easily as if I were a cockroach.

He could pull my arms off my body; he could strangle me with one hand; he could fly me out to the ocean and drop me in the middle of the Atlantic; and if he really wanted to, he could fly me above one of the church steeples in nearby East Rock and impale me.

Hell, even if I had a gun and I was able to shoot him, the motherfucker could heal.

"You're one of them," he finally said. "A normal. There is nothing special or unique about you. I am a different class of human, as are Veronique and Sabine. As are the others. Your life has little significance to us and the future we will bring."

"Did you say there were others?"

"Surely you knew we weren't the only ones," he said, his voice filled with melancholy.

"I figured there would be more, but I really had no idea. I'm still new at all this; I'm still uncovering all the details. I have to be honest with you, Angel."

"You know my name?"

"Grace told me – I mean, Sabine. But she wants to be called Grace now."

"Sabine is mischievous, and it was better when she was kept away from others. Veronique's actions have come as a surprise. She never indicated before that she was unhappy. What an incredibly stupid girl."

"That's your opinion," I said, my voice growing with confidence. I quickly stomped that confidence out like it was a small fire. Now was the time to be modest, not to try to have a dick measuring contest with a superhuman. "But everyone has opinions."

"You are right about that." He nodded and walked back over to me. "You are the weakest man I've ever met, and I've met many pathetic scientists. It amazes me that Sabine and Veronique have joined forces with you. That just shows how truly warped their minds are."

"They are allowed to make their own decisions," I said through gritted teeth.

"You said you wanted to be honest with me. What is it exactly that you want to be honest about?" he asked, settling his black eyes on me. "The gunfire has stopped down there, so make this quick."

"I know you're not going to believe this, but I am trying to expose this facility, expose what these people have done."

I was glad he couldn't read my mind. Not only did I want to expose the facility, but I wanted to *destroy* it. This was one detail Grace and I hadn't worked out; it was something we were going to play by ear if we had the opportunity. The most important thing was to save Veronique.

Below us, a man screamed.

Angel smirked. "You are feeling confident?"

"Honestly, I don't know what I'm feeling. Just a few days ago I was a regular guy, and now look at me."

He shook his head. "You shouldn't have gotten involved. You could have lived your pathetic life until your natural death; now your death will come rapidly, tonight. It is rather funny, isn't it?"

"But I did, and I needed something – some *change* … something to make my life have meaning. So, I don't regret it. There, I said it. What's happened here at this place is wrong; people shouldn't experiment on other people. Didn't we learn that in the 1940s and 50s? We shouldn't do this. You shouldn't …"

"I shouldn't what?"

293

"You shouldn't exist," I said, fire burning deep within me. "You're an amalgamation of a human, you are ..."

"I agree with you, Gideon." He crouched before me. "I am an amalgamation of a human. But you're not being honest."

"What do you mean?"

"How much of what you are doing is driven by desire?"

"Desire?"

I hadn't really thought of it in that way, and as I sat there staring at him, I realized that he may be right. There were many desires at play. My desire for Grace, for Veronique, for power, my desire to matter, to make a difference, to become a famous writer.

"I see it in your eyes, Gideon, you have ulterior motives."

He picked me up with one hand and body slammed me to the ground. I felt the concrete beneath me give way slightly, the wind rush out of me.

"This is for your own good, Gideon," he said as he loomed over me.

"I'm trying to do something here," I pleaded with him. "Everyone has an ulterior motive."

"You've just now figured that out? This is a poor time to learn a new lesson."

"Just a week ago I was nobody. And I'm still nobody!" I shouted, my breath barely holding on after being slammed on my back. "But at least I tried … At least I tried to do something different than the others. Yeah, I know what you mean by others. Everyone is an other. You and I are …"

"We?" he took a step back.

"Yeah, Angel, we have a similarity."

He started to laugh, and as if he were some type of weather god, droplets of rain began to fall from the sky.

"Let me rephrase, Angel, we *had* a similarity."

Something twisted inside my body. I rolled over and pushed myself up, eventually getting to my knees, and then my feet. More rain fell, quickly saturating my lab coat.

I had to keep my legs wide to stand up, but I did it, and as I stood I pointed at him.

A smirk formed on his face as the rain beat down upon us. "Say your piece, and then I will end it."

"My piece? I was like you one week ago, Angel, playing a role, fitting into whatever *they* wanted me to do. Following their rules, obeying their laws, doing what they said was right, avoiding what they said was wrong. And then I became like me," I growled.

"Are you suggesting that you are no longer a conformist?" he asked, moving his wet hair out of his face.

"I'm suggesting more than that. I'm no one's bitch any longer. Do you see now? There is a difference between us now."

Angel had me by the throat in a matter of seconds, only to be broadsided by a long metal pole.

He dropped me. I landed on my knees and scurried away, my heart pounding in my chest. I couldn't believe what I'd just done.

Bullets, hundreds of them, tore into Angel's skin.

They pierced his flesh, ripped through his black armor, and worse, as soon as they exploded out of him from behind they turned in the air and came back around again.

He staggered to the left, and to my horror, I saw that a few of the wounds on his face had already started to heal.

That was when he was thrown sideways, an invisible force stopping him just before he reached the edge of the building and smacking his head against the parapet.

Angel was out cold, oblivious to the rain slapping against his body.

"Holy shit ..."

Grace and Veronique stood at the opposite end of the roof. Neither seemed hurt, but Veronique did have a slight lean to her, as if she were quickly running out of juice.

"We have to destroy the place," I said, cursing myself for not getting a few gallons of gasoline earlier.

"But how?" Grace asked. "We need to leave before he wakes up."

"No." I shook my head. "We destroy the place with him on top of it."

Chapter Twenty-Seven: Goodbye, Cruel World

Veronique came up with one hell of an idea. She moved slowly over to Angel and knelt before him as her hand flashed red.

His energy became hers and as she drained him, his skin started to dry and wither, blips of red light cascading up her arms. The energy formed a sphere over the crown of her head as the rain continued to fall from the sky, forming small puddles on the rooftop.

A look of realization spread across Grace's face.

"It's brilliant," she said, and her eyes flashed white. Using her psychokinetic ability, Grace began to move the ball of light and energy away from Veronique's head.

Once she was sure she could do it, she returned the pulsing red sphere to Veronique, who absorbed even more energy from Angel's body.

Call it dormant kinetic energy, or simply a ball of combustible matter – whatever it was, the sphere she was forming continued to enlarge until it became the size of a beach ball. She continued to drain

Angel, his skin shriveling and turning black and blue, his eyes sinking into his skull, his limbs becoming frail.

"We have to get out of here before you drop that thing," I told Grace.

I could already hear a helicopter, and I knew reinforcements were on the way.

As Veronique finished up, I walked to the edge of the building and looked down.

I wasn't prepared for what I saw.

The secret agent men were scattered, dead or dying, their bodies arranged in a way that resembled a black rainbow of carnage. There were severed limbs, pools of blood drummed upon by the rain, a few men wheezing as they tried to keep their intestines from spilling out, and one, toward the back, was sobbing, a shredded torso in his arms.

"Oh my god ..."

The butterflies in my stomach shifted when my body rose into the air.

I glanced over my shoulder to see Grace controlling my body, lifting me up and over the edge of the rooftop.

She and Veronique were already airborne, hovering just a few feet above the ground. It was amazing how much her power had improved, especially since she was also in control of our bodies and a sphere of blistering red light, now the size of one of those large exercise balls.

The sphere hung like a disco ball above us, and as Grace lowered all of us to the ground, the sphere remained in place.

Like a floating lantern, it hovered, casting an eerie crimson glow on our surroundings as we turned and made our way toward our getaway vehicle.

I had a strange awareness that we were minutes away from encountering more hostile forces. The feeling of urgency was new to me, but something I would start to get going forward. I'd read about soldiers being able to sense an oncoming battle and now I knew what that felt like.

Crazy, but I knew they were coming.

The guy in black mil-spec armor who had waived us in earlier now hung out of the check-in station, a portion of his arm cut away by a slice of steel Veronique had peeled off of the building.

"Are we ready to do this?" I asked them.

Veronique nodded, a predatory grin stretching across her face. All Grace could muster was a tight smile.

"This is what we came here for," I reminded her. "Remember what they did to you, remember what they put you through. Blow that fucking building to the ground."

With a deep breath in, Grace cast her hands out before her. The large sphere of red energy whooshed toward the building, bursting through the front entrance like a cannonball.

"We need to run," she said, grabbing my hand.

The three of us started to bolt as we saw the sphere of energy lift up through the building, briefly splashing the air with a dazzling array of lights before turning around and heading downward, toward the basement, the hyperloop pod, the subrooms that were used to keep people captive.

We reached the Tacoma when the explosion rocked the sky.

It shook the ground, causing car alarms to go off, electricity to flash, the power grid to shut down.

"Drive, Chip," I said as soon as we got into the vehicle.

It was already running, the windshield wipers going a mile a minute. He took off before Veronique could even get the door shut, navigating over the slick streets toward our other getaway vehicle.

I reached over and pulled her door shut. Veronique's tight body now pressed into mine, Grace between Chip and me.

I would later have nightmares when remembering the Rose-Lyle facility, and as many others had done before me, I would bottle those nightmares up and cast them into the sea of troubled memories.

PTSD? Sure, I would experience that too.

But I'd also experienced what it felt like to be a changed man, to have one's reality completely turned on them, the rug pulled out from beneath them, a mallet of truth cracked against their skull.

I would come to like the new me.

It only took him a few minutes to get us to the Dodge. We transferred vehicles, I threw the peace sign at Chip, and revved the Charger's engine.

Fire trucks raced in the other direction as we approached the on-ramp to the highway. We were going to head west, to see what else was out there, and hopefully, to shut down more of those laboratories.

Once we got on the wet highway and were about forty miles away from New Haven, I put the Charger on auto drive. I gasped, exhaled audibly, and relaxed in my seat.

Grace was next to me, a tight grin on her face. Veronique was asleep in the back, her hair and body still wet.

I knew I wasn't superpowered, regardless of the pictures I'd discovered on Grace's drive. I didn't have any ability, and I wasn't going to be able to help them in that way. I was sure of this, but that didn't make me weak.

Angel was wrong about me being weak, and now, he was likely dead.

But there will be others, Grace said inside my head.

I know, I thought back.

My phone buzzed, and I checked the message as the Charger continued along the highway.

Luke: Are you all right?

Me: Yeah ... We got out of there okay.

Luke: We can video chat about it.

Me: It's only going to get more complicated from here.

Luke: I'll say! Have you checked your sales ranking yet?

Me: Nope, I've been too busy getting accosted by a superpowered guy named Angel.

Luke: I don't know what that means, but it sounds crazy.

Me: It'll be in book two.

Luke: Do I have to send you a screenshot? Check your rankings!

I clicked on the EBAYmazon app on my phone and brought it up. I went to the search bar, pressed it once and said the name of the title, "Mutants in the Making."

It took my phone a moment to show me the results, but I saw the orange tag next to my book title that said 'Bestseller' before the cover finished loading.

"No way," I said as my phone refreshed, telling me I had several messages in my inbox.

Two of them concerned me the most.

One was from an anonymous sender, evident by the title of their email address: Throwaway_NewHaven@googleface.com.

Gideon Caldwell,

I know Subject S and Subject V are with you. I worked with S for several years at the Rose-Lyle facility. Please respond to my email with a number where I may reach you. I don't want you to think I'm trying to track you. I'm not, so please get a fake number or use some type of phone number forwarding service. There are plenty available.

--KK

The other was from a man named David Butler.

Gideon,

I read your book and loved it. To cut right to the chase, I know about a similar experiment going on in Austin, Texas. Please let me know if this information interests you by replying to this email. We can discuss more when we meet in person. I'll also send some pictures soon.

"Can we find a place to sleep?" Grace asked me.

"Sure. It'll be another hour before we're out of Connecticut, and we can find a place to stay in New York. Somewhere nice."

Chapter Twenty-Eight: Cherry Blossom Girls, Inc.

We took a big left when we got to Port Chester, saying goodbye to I-95. Besides, we weren't heading to New York City. As I let the car auto drive, I reread the message from the guy in Texas, David Butler. I sent him a reply, fishing for more info, wondering if I could possibly get a few more details before I headed down south.

But I knew in my heart that was where we were heading; we had to go south to eventually go west. If Texas didn't pan out, we could hide out in Santa Fe for a few days as the emails came in, as I was able to verify things a little further.

I also needed to start the second installment of the *Mutants in the Making* series.

The second installment would cover what happened after Angel first showed up. So, in a way, it was a living document, because what "happened" was what was currently happening.

I decided not to reply to the scientist at the Rose-Lyle facility. I had a feeling about him, and opening up a dialogue didn't seem to be in our best interest.

I was, however, happy to see that my book had already reached someone there. Even if they lobbied EBAYmazon to shut down the book, it would still be out there, and it would still reach an audience, either through illegal downloads on a torrent site or with people posting the book online in blog format.

I also had a feeling this wouldn't be the last I heard from the scientist, and boy, would I turn out to be right.

Goodbye New York, hello New Jersey.

I would need gas at some point in the future, but we could get it after we passed New Jersey, sometime tomorrow. They still pumped the gas for you in New Jersey, something that's always weirded me out. Not that the gas attendant would care if there was a woman passed out in the back.

Still, the lower profile we kept, the better.

Gideon 'Low Profile' Caldwell.

Grace laughed.

"I thought we had a thing about reading my thoughts."

"They are just so loud."

Damn, I thought as we pulled up to the Marriott in Hanover, New Jersey, *we need to get some type of discount card for this chain.*

Which made no sense, seeing as how we hadn't spent a dime to stay in the place.

Thoughts like that would come to me every now and again. Even with the situation I was in, it was still hard for me not to think the way I used to about goods and services.

"And what shall we say this time?" Grace hadn't spoken much during the ride, aside from an occasional comment on my thoughts. She focused instead on the lights along the highway, the vehicles, and something we were listening to on NPR.

Ira Glass again.

I should go on *This American Life*.

Was there anything more American than what I had just done over the last few days, risking it all for one big payday, an uncertain future?

I'm not saying I was some sort of Lewis and Clark, but I definitely wasn't a loser sci-fi writer who worked at a Yale gift shop that sold lamps any longer.

I considered that for a moment. "Let's go with *she's drunk again*. We're business people – no, look what I'm wearing … we're scientists … No, we're doctors – hell yes, we're doctors. We work for a biomedical company called Cherry Blossom Girls, Inc. And she's drunk. She's a drunk nurse."

"Girls?"

"Or boys. I don't know. It's the name that came to me. Nothing sexist or anything. We could be Cherry Blossom Non-Binaries, if you like that."

"Girls is okay, as long as you don't mind it."

"We can go by the abbreviation too. CBG. It has a ring to it."

I looked in my rearview mirror at Veronique, who lay sideways in the backseat, still in the scrubs and lab coat we'd put on her. She was dry now, but her hair was a bit matted.

"That sounds like a pretty good plan," Grace said in Ira Glass's voice. "You should probably take your military helmet off."

"Shit, I forgot about that." I removed the remains of my helmet. "But regarding our strategy, no one's going to care anyway. Your powers are incredible. Just fry all their brains if they try to get in our way."

She raised an eyebrow at me. "Fry all their brains?"

"I'm kidding, please don't do that unless we really need to get rid of someone."

The things I said now that I had broken bad …

"Okay, I'll only fry brains if necessary," Grace said as her body morphed from her base form to her geisha form.

We parked the Dodge Charger – no valet here – and I lifted Veronique into my arms. Grace took my duffle bag from the back seat, and without further ado, we entered the lobby of the Marriott Hanover.

I pity the fool who looked over at us and instantly had their mind wiped by Grace.

There were only a few people in the lobby anyway: the receptionist and a family that had just checked in and were waiting for the husband to park the car.

"We'd like your best room," Grace said to the receptionist, offering him a curt smile. "Two beds, and we have a reservation. Should be under the name Edward King or possibly our company, Cherry Blossom Girls, Inc."

"Let me just see here …" the mustached clerk said as he clickety-clicked on the mouse. "Found it. Edward and Jill King, CBG, INC. Great. Let me just prepare your room key and you should be good to go."

As he went to work, I took one more look around the lobby.

This place wasn't as tall as the Marriott we'd stayed at in Stamford, but what it lacked in height it made up for with space. It was expansive, with red carpets and orange accents, plenty of seating areas and plush leather couches, glass countertops near the continental breakfast area, and of course some generic, yet warm, art.

About a minute later, we took our elevator up to the suite on the top floor.

It was one of those mirrored elevators, and it was a little strange for me to see myself – head shaved, scar on face, bruised, and carrying Veronique in my arms – next to Grace in her Asian female doctor form with her bangs cut high and tight, cute glasses, and dimples.

We found our room and the lights came on automatically.

The suite was nice, and it had two queen-sized beds facing a large television that sat on a long wooden table. Near the floor-to-ceiling windows were two sofas and a reading nook. Next to the second queen-sized bed was a writing desk.

Damn, I needed a beer.

Luckily, the room had a mini fridge and refreshments on top. No beer, but I did down one of those small bottles of whiskey.

"We need to get her some new clothes," I told Grace as she morphed back into her base form.

"We can get some tomorrow." She sat on the edge of the bed and crossed one leg over the next. "Also, a new car."

"I was just thinking that. We'll need to switch out cars daily. It shouldn't be hard." I moved to the writing desk to set up my laptop. "We'll just trade whatever car we have with the person whose car we're taking. To throw anyone tracking us off, we'll alternate that with simply giving the vehicle to whatever random person we see. We have a ton of cash. Maybe we'll buy a used car too."

I opened my laptop and clicked on the EBAYmazon direct publishing dashboard.

I gulped, the blood rushing to my head as I saw the incredible day I'd had.

I'd sold three hundred books over the last twelve hours and had over one hundred thousand page reads.

It's not fucking possible.

Even though I'd seen the 'Bestseller' tag, my hand shook as I refreshed the data to make sure it wasn't a dream.

Nope, that's what you've done so far today, I thought.

Sure, the sales were at $0.99, but I had a feeling my bank accounts would be tracked anyway and besides, I had unlimited access to cash with Grace around. The book was getting out there, finding a wider audience, and that was all that mattered. Whatever magic Luke had worked had fundamentally changed the sales trajectory of my book.

I clicked the link to part one of *Mutants in the Making* to see that I was ranked in the top one thousand, no small feat considering the millions upon millions of ebooks that were published. EBAYmazon had made it so easy to publish an e-book, and self-publishing had become so widely accepted, that by 2030 everyone and their dog had a book out.

The highest I'd ever been before was the top two hundred fifty thousand.

"Great job," Grace said, relaxing onto the bed and turning on the TV. She found a home improvement show and increased the volume. "I think your ranking will improve tomorrow."

"Maybe," I said, not wanting to jinx myself.

I checked my emails again and saw that I'd received another one from David Butler in Austin, Texas. This one had pictures of a facility near a body of water.

I clicked through the photos, not really finding anything that would cement the fact that it was a facility used for the experiments.

Then I looked through some PDFs he'd attached about the people guarding the facility. It was definitely MercSecure, the same group guarding the now-defunct Rose-Lyle facility. Thinking of that name reminded me of the ring of dead guards I'd seen when I looked over the rooftop.

Damn, I thought, trying to swallow that memory. Of course, attempting to suppress a memory only created another one.

I saw Angel in my mind's eye, his skin shriveled, the look of death on his face. He was likely dead. There was no way he could have survived that blast.

I took a deep breath and clicked through more photos. Nope, there wasn't concrete evidence that this was a similar facility to the one that we'd just destroyed.

That was, until I found a photo of a group of men and women entering the facility.

Almost all of the people were slightly blurred in the photo. The one person in focus was a slightly older scientist with thinning white hair. He wore a tie, glasses with white frames, and a shaved head.

He also had the requisite lab coat on.

I would have clicked through to the next photo if there hadn't been directions on the photo to *"Show it to one of the supers."*

"Hey, Grace," I said, bringing my laptop over to her. "Does this person look familiar to you?"

She shook her head and returned her attention to the screen, where they were ripping out the foundation from an old Boston brownstone.

I was just about to move back to the desk when Grace gasped.

"What is it?" I asked.

She tore the laptop from my hands and touched the screen to zoom in on the image.

She wasn't focused on the man; however, she *was* focused on the partially blurred woman who stood next to him.

"It's her," Grace said with a certainty I seldom heard from her.

"Her?"

"The founder …" She glanced over at Veronique. "Mother."

Everything came to me at once, aided by some of Grace's psychic powers. I saw this woman throughout her life – images only though, as Grace was never actually allowed to meet her.

I then *heard* the woman speaking to Grace, and realized that she *had* actually met her, but that Grace had been blindfolded, which meant she couldn't link to the person.

"All of you are my sons and daughters," Mother had whispered to her. "But you are my favorite."

I took a step back.

I figured Grace would be distraught, but the act of transferring this experience to me seemed to have calmed her. She returned her attention to the television program while I clicked through more photos, saving the photo of Mother to my desktop.

"She was in Austin," I told her after I snapped my laptop shut. "That's where we're going."

Grace nodded, a determined look on her face. "That's fine."

Realizing that checking my sales numbers again wouldn't really prove anything, I placed my laptop back in my duffle bag and took out my sleep clothes. One sniff at my armpit and I figured a shower was in order.

I entered the bathroom, turned on the hot water and waited to see just how hot it would get before I took off my clothes. Once I was satisfied with the temperature, I stepped in and let the water spray against my face.

My thoughts traced over the day, from the morning planning session to the assault on the Rose-Lyle facility. The important thing was that we had Veronique, and we had a plan. I'd never been to Texas – never been south of the Mason-Dixon line, actually – but it seemed like a viable next step.

We needed to get to Texas and we needed to find out more about Mother.

Changing locations and vehicles would make us harder to track. That said, there must have been some type of tracking device embedded in each woman; otherwise, they wouldn't have eventually found us at the hotel in Stamford. We had to keep on the move and stick to public locations.

As the water turned my skin red, I thought about the message I'd received from the scientist who worked at the Rose-Lyle facility. There was more to this message, but I was still uncertain whether we should start up a dialogue. I needed to speak to Grace about him and figure out if he really was one of the scientists that would interview her.

Again, something to do later.

I nearly slipped and cracked my head on the tiled wall when the bathroom curtain was pulled aside.

I was greeted by a naked woman, story of my goddamn life.

"Veronique?" I asked, déjà vu slapping me in the face like a motherfucker.

"Any room for me in there? I'm feeling dirty." She was completely nude, her nipples erect, and a perfectly straight line shaved in her pubes …

She was clean-shaven last time. And hadn't there been a birthmark?

"Just kidding." Veronique's face folded, starting from the middle, and Grace's unique, Scandinavian features formed. Her hair grew in length, her dark eyes turned blue, and the change cascaded down her body, her breasts increasing in size, her hips widening.

"That's a terrible joke," I said. "A terrible, terrible joke. Don't do that again."

"Too many rules," she said playfully as she got into the shower with me. "No reading your mind, no changing into your mom, and no changing into Veronique." She turned to me and wrapped her arms around my neck. "Anything else you'd like to add to that?"

"No, we're good for now."

I thought of the long day ahead, the fact that we were under threat, and the additional details emerging from Texas.

"Quiet, Writer Gideon, just enjoy it while it lasts," Grace said as she moved in to kiss me.

The end.

Reader,

Writing this book has been an immense pleasure for me. I really want this series to reach as many people as possible, and the better the response, the faster I'll get the books out.

Please take a moment to review the book and tell other readers what you liked about it. After all, your reviews are what drive all my series and encourage me to really let loose and explore.

You can find out about more Harem Lit books (like this book) on the Facebook page.

You can also join the Proxima Galaxy here to see how all my books are connected and get early copies of my new works for free!

--Harmon Cooper

If you didn't know, "Luke" in this book is based on a real Canadian writer friend of mine, whose book above is a beloved LitRPG series. Please check it out if you haven't already!